Dead Trees

Brent Saltzman

Text copyright © 2017 by Brent Saltzman

DEAD TREES

All rights reserved.

ISBN-13: 978-0692992104

ISBN-10: 0692992103

10 9 8 5 7 6 3 2 1 05 06 07 08 09

Printed in the U.S.A.
First American Edition: November 2017

To L

"The nose of a mob is its imagination. By this, at any time, it can be quietly led."

Edgar Allan Poe

In 1645, England is in the midst of a civil war.

Disease, famine, and death stalk the land.

People are desperate.

People are scared.

And people are looking for someone to blame.

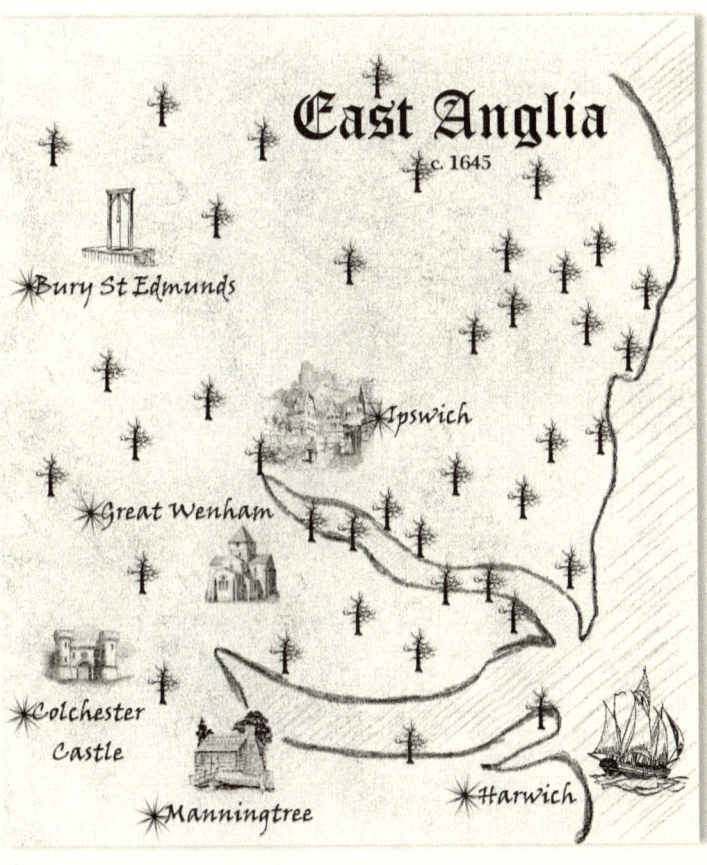

East Anglia

c. 1645

Bury St Edmunds

Ipswich

Great Wenham

Colchester
Castle

Manningtree

Harwich

-1-

DEVIL'S MARKS

MARCH 1645

Flaming shadows of a dying fire danced upon the stone walls of Elizabeth Clarke's tiny home. The winter had not been kind to her village, nestled within the heart of Essex on the eastern border of England. *This war has been kind to no one*, Elizabeth reminded herself as she heaved a log into her fireplace, throwing up a light cloud of ash and embers. Indeed, the civil war that had been ravaging the country had already hit the nation's citizens hard. Disease, famine, and violence had been rippling through the land for months. The cold seemed to claim another life at least once a week.

These were dark times.

But I am here, Elizabeth Clarke would tell herself.

The fact that she was alive and healthy was a testament to her perseverance. At 80 years old, she was already well past the age that many poor were expected to live; even the nobility rarely reached 70. On top of that, her right leg had been amputated years ago—in fact she could no longer remember how long it had been. She had been using a flimsy wooden prosthetic for so long that she no longer noticed how it clacked on stone floors or left splinters in her bed.

As Elizabeth Clarke sat down and prepared to retire for the evening, she was greeted by a tiny visitor in the form of one of the several stray cats that occasionally wandered into her home. She let it affectionately rub against her wooden leg then gave it a pat on the head before tossing it a piece of cold beef. She didn't mind the cats. While a woman who preferred the silence of solitude, she was still prone to the occasional bouts of loneliness. The stray cats helped keep those feelings at bay. Besides, she preferred them over the company of other people. Elizabeth Clarke *hated* other people, and they hated her because she had little qualm with making her feelings known…quite frequently.

Which is why she found herself so annoyed when a gentle knock on her front door scared the stray cat into fleeing out of sight.

"Who's there?" Elizabeth Clarke asked, taking no caution to hide her sour tone. She really, truly, did *not* like visitors. Especially at such late hours.

There was no answer.

Grumbling, Elizabeth Clarke clambered over and put her ear to the door. On the other side, she heard low, muffled singing: "*There was a ship that sailed, on the Lowland Sea. And the name of his ship, was Golden Vanity.*"

"Who's out there?!" Elizabeth Clarke called again.

The singing continued. "*And we feared she would be taken, by the fearsome enemy. As she sailed through the waves, of the Lowland Sea.*"

Frustrated now, Elizabeth Clarke grumbled and opened the door. Behind it, standing out in the cold night, was her beautiful 15-year-old neighbor, Rebecca West.

"Good evening, Ms. Clarke," Rebecca said with a smile. Elizabeth Clarke *hated* that smile as much as she hated the girl. "It's quite chilly."

"What do you want?"

"I'm afraid we've run out of flour. My mother has asked if we'd to borrow some. She promises to replenish you at the market in two days, with extra."

"Fine." Elizabeth Clarke went to retrieve the flour from her cupboard while Rebecca West followed her inside. Clarke didn't like the young woman, nor her mother, Anne West. She didn't like how she was always parading around with young men from the village; a different one every week, it seemed. *God does not approve of harlotry.* Nonetheless, Elizabeth Clarke wasn't completely heartless, and also knew the faster she sacrificed some flour, the faster the pretty young thing would be out of her house.

Rebecca West had what one might call a delightful disposition. She was always cheery. Always smiling. Always radiating innocence.

Elizabeth Clarke didn't like it.

There was something artificial about the girl's smile. Something sinister. She knew the girl was simply disguising her sinful behavior behind a veil of purity. But Elizabeth Clarke found comfort in knowing that one day the girl would answer to God.

And God sees past every mask.

Elizabeth Clarke finally retrieved the flour but nearly leapt off her foot when she saw the large, gray *rat* perched casually on Rebecca West's shoulders. The rodent gently tussled the girl's hair.

"Vermin!" Elizabeth Clarke shouted, clutching her chest. "Get that filthy creature out of my house!"

"He's harmless," Rebecca assured the old woman. She reached up and stroked her pet rat's fur. Rebecca West had kept the rodent as a pet for years and was rarely seen without it, but Elizabeth Clarke was certain that the young woman would have the common decency not to bring such a disease-riddled creature into her home.

"It's vile! Take your flour and get out!"

Rebecca thanked the old woman and left, leaving her alone. Elizabeth Clarke sat, still coming down from short breaths, clouds of frosty air escaping her lips. *I'm 80 years old, if I didn't know any better, I'd say she was* trying *to scare me to death with that ghastly beast!*

After a few minutes, she finally managed to calm down, before there was yet *another* knock on the door.

What does she want now?!

Elizabeth Clarke swung the door open, fully expecting to see the infuriatingly-nubile face of Rebecca West. Instead, she was met by the charming smile of a bearded man in a top hat and cape. He could have been no older than his late 20s, though his rugged physique may have suggested otherwise. His eyes twinkled like the Devil's himself in the moonlight as his long black coat extended down toward his tall boots. He carried a leather satchel that reminded her of the doctor's bags they carried when they made house calls.

He was dressed like the kind of dashing gentleman Elizabeth may have pursued in her younger days. And he spoke like one, too, "Good evening, ma'am." The man tipped his hat. "I do hope we are not disturbing you."

"Who are you?" Elizabeth looked over the man's shoulder. Behind him, another man stood. This man was ten years older and balding. He was accompanied by four women, all in coats, who looked like teenagers.

"Ah, how rude of me!" the young man exclaimed

cheerily. "My name is Matthew Hopkins. This is my associate, Mr. John Stearne, and our four lovely assistants, Ms. Mary Phillips, Pricilla Briggs, Frances Milles and Elizabeth Hunt. Elizabeth is such a pretty name, don't you think, Ms. Clarke? Or do you still prefer to go by Mrs? I understand that you are a widow, and I shan't wish to offend."

"I go by *piss off*," Elizabeth Clarke said as she attempted to slam the door shut.

However, Matthew Hopkins coolly placed his satchel in position between the door and the frame, preventing her from closing it. "I'm afraid," he said, the facade of sweetness quickly fading from his voice, "that we have official orders from the magistrate. You have two options, Ms. Clarke. You can cooperate and get this finished quickly so we can all curl up and go to sleep on this cold night. *Or* you can resist. And make this evening much more difficult for all parties involved."

After a few seconds, Elizabeth Clarke relented and opened the door. "What do you people want?"

"May we enter your home, Ms. Clarke?" Matthew Hopkins asked, the devilish smile returning.

"Guess I've got naught a choice if the magistrate's involved," she muttered. "Come in. But don't get too comfortable. I'm tired." She hobbled over to the fireplace and put on another log as the six visitors filed in, closing the door behind them.

Matthew Hopkins calmly placed his satchel on Elizabeth Clarke's table and opened it wide, shuffling through its contents as he spoke. "Are you aware of the strange happenings around the village lately, Ms. Clarke?"

"I'm aware of the strange happenings across all this bloody land," she replied grumpily. "Young people killing each other over disagreements on how to worship God. Ridiculous."

"Perhaps." Hopkins shrugged his shoulders. "Perhaps not. How one chooses to worship God is of no consequence to me. However, what *is* important to me is that one is not communing with the enemy of God."

Elizabeth Clarke went cold. She gulped, suddenly realizing who these people were. Their silence only confirmed the truth of which she was suddenly, and horrifyingly, aware.

"Do you understand what I am saying, Ms.

Clarke?" Hopkins asked as he pulled a razorblade, glinting in the moonlight that shined in through the windows, out of his bag. He handed the deadly-looking blade to one of the female assistants.

"Answer him, you demon!" John Stearne barked, his voice like gravel, no doubt ravaged by decades of tobacco and alcohol.

"Now, now, John," Matthew Hopkins looked at his associate, "aggression is the enemy of progress." He turned to Elizabeth Clarke. "Ms. Clarke, you have been formally accused of witchcraft."

"I've done *no* such thing!" she seethed. "Magic and hocus pocus is fantasy!"

Matthew Hopkins smiled. "Ms. Clarke, you seem to have an archaic understanding of what I mean when I say 'witchcraft.' I speak not of broomsticks and potions, here. No, no. However, it seems that several villagers have the sneaking suspicion that you have made a deal with the Devil to get your way. And this is treason, ma'am. Not only against your country, but against your God."

Elizabeth Clarke was shook. She knew exactly what they were talking about. "The…the child…" she said, her words trembling as the realization struck her swiftly and painfully. "The child...but...I swear, I had nothing to do with it! It was just...it was just coincidence!"

Matthew Hopkins clasped his hands together, nodded to his assistants, and grinned at the old woman. "My dear, there is no such thing as coincidence."

Elizabeth Clarke's eyes darted back and forth in a panic as three of the four women grabbed her and held her down. John Stearne approached and began ripping off the old woman's clothes until she was completely nude, her frail body exposed to the cold.

"Let go of me!" she cried as loudly as she could.

"Cooperation will ensure speedy proof of innocence, Ms. Clarke," Hopkins said as his last female assistant approached the old woman, brandishing the razorblade.

"Are you going to kill me?!"

"Heavens, no!" Hopkins almost looked offended. "We're not savages! We kill no one, not even witches. We leave that for the courts to decide."

The assistant with the razorblade, who Elizabeth Clarke recognized as Mary Phillips, approached slowly but purposefully. She held the blade high. There was a bloodlust in the young woman's eyes. A sadistic grin crossed her face.

"Now," Matthew Hopkins said, approaching the old woman, "it is my sincerest belief, Ms. Clarke, that you are an *innocent* woman. So, give us a chance to prove your innocence. Please, do not squirm."

Mary Phillips raised the blade to Elizabeth Clarke's neck. The old woman closed her tear-filled eyes and began to pray in Latin as the young assistant pressed the razor to her skin and ran it down her neck, slicing off a patch of thin, graying hair. Mary Phillips worked like a surgeon, going over every inch of the old woman's body and removing any shred of body hair she could find.

"You see, Ms. Clarke, as you are hopefully *un*aware, one that is in league with the Devil and thus is guilty of the crime of treason and witchcraft never works alone. They must use agents, usually in the form of small animals, to assist with their evil bidding. These are called Familiars, as, again, you *hopefully* do *not* know. And they cannot subsist on the normal food like bread or meat that you or I partake in. Instead, these Familiars require sustenance in the form of life energy, which they are given by their host witch."

Matthew Hopkins slipped on a pair of glasses and leaned down before Elizabeth Clarke, who was beginning to look defeated. She stared at the ceiling, crying in agony as Hopkins examined her body.

"When the Familiars feed off their host witch, they leave behind a mark. A Devil's Mark. Just…like…" he found a small mole on Elizabeth Clarke's thigh. Four of them, in fact, all forming a peculiar circle. "…these."

"I've had those forever!" Elizabeth Clarke protested. "Please, sir! I'm not—"

Just then, there was a commotion at one of the open windows. One of the stray cats, whom Elizabeth Clarke had regularly fed, leapt inside to escape the chill of the outside world. Then another, and another, until four cats looked on curiously at the strange visitors to the domain they often called their own.

Hopkins' eyes went wide. "Four Imps [alternative to Familiars, often used interchangeably], four marks." He smiled and looked at Elizabeth Clarke. "Do you still want to tell me that this is just coincidence?"

"They're just strays!" Elizabeth wheezed.

"What are their names?"

"They don't have names!"

"All witches give their Familiars names," Hopkins said. "Please, humor me."

"I'm not a witch and they don't have–"

"*What are their names?!*" Hopkins exploded, shouting in Elizabeth's crying face, grabbing the razorblade from Mary Phillips and holding it to the old woman's neck.

"I don't know! Please!"

Hopkins looked back at the cats. They looked confused but not overly alarmed. Hopkins found their lack of fear, frankly, insulting. He turned back to Elizabeth. "Names. *Now.*"

Panicking, Elizabeth looked around the room and named the cats. "Vinegar Tom, Sack and Sugar,

Jamara, and, uh…"

"Name the last Imp, witch!" Hopkins squeezed the blade tight. It trembled in his grip.

"Holt!" Elizabeth cried. "My last Imp's name is Holt!"

Hopkins smiled and stood up, glancing at his compatriots. "Did everyone hear that?"

"Aye," John Stearne nodded. "She admitted they were her Imps."

"That she did." Hopkins licked his lips menacingly. "That she did."

Minutes later, after allowing Elizabeth Clarke to dress, the witch hunters dragged her out into the cold and stuffed her into the back of their carriage as she cried in dissent. Then, they began the short trek across the village to Colchester Castle, where the poor old woman would be imprisoned until her trial for witchcraft.

A trial that would set in motion a chain of events that would change the world forever.

-2-
BELLS AND INCENSE

AUGUST 1647

The girl could have been no more than seven years old. She lied in bed peacefully surrounded by family as her last breaths came in long, difficult gasps. Sweat beaded down her forehead, the final stages of the deadly fever as it prepared to take her life. On one side of her bed, her father held her sobbing mother. On the other side sat a man in formal clergy robes. He was one year from 40 and clean cut with short brown hair and a strong build.

The minister, John Gaule, stroked the child's head and sang to her a ballad from his childhood.

"I'm afraid," the child said, her voice weak.

"I know," John Gaule replied. He took his free hand and grabbed one of hers. He held tight. "But you don't need to be. The world, the one beyond the veil, is a beautiful world. Full of colors and light and love. Have you ever heard the story of the princess and the peasant?"

The little girl shook her head. She was fading. Fast.

Her parents knew it. The husband held his wife tighter as their child prepared to take her final breaths.

John Gaule told the story. "There was a princess. She was beautiful, kind, compassionate. But she had a secret. Every night, she would lock herself in her tower and not emerge till the following morning. No one knew why she did this, but no one really cared. Everyone loved her. Especially a lowly peasant. But the peasant knew he could never be with her. So he kept his distance. Never getting too close.

"Well, one night, a sparrow came to the peasant's window. The creature seemed friendly, so the peasant followed it into the woods where, as the sun rose, it transformed into the princess. See, the princess had been cursed long ago. She was doomed to live as a sparrow every single night.

"But there was a way to lift the curse, you see. The

peasant, if he so chose, could have the curse transferred unto him, thus taking on its burden and freeing the princess."

"Did he do it?" the little girl asked.

"Yes," John Gaule said. "He took her curse and freed her."

"Why?"

"Because he loved her. And this love, this unconditional care for another, is something that you are surrounded with right now. And in the next world, you will feel it always. God will take care of you. He will take on your curses, child. He will take your sickness. He will take your pain. And you will live in His kingdom forever, and you will be happy."

"Do you promise?"

"Yes," Gaule said. "I promise."

Ten minutes later, John Gaule left the little girl's bedroom at her parents' home and stepped out into the hall. It was here, away from the prying eyes of others, where he slumped to the floor and cried. It was never easy watching someone die. Especially a child.

What a waste, he thought.

Here was a life, full of promise and potential, extinguished before it had a chance to blossom into something wonderful.

For a moment, he considered condemning the very God he worshipped for such a cruel act. But after taking a few deep breaths, he regained his composure, stood up, and left, walking the few blocks back to his church. In his office, his assistant, Daniel, was busy writing letters.

"How did it go?" Daniel asked.

Gaule plopped down at his desk on the other side of the small room. "She's with God, now."

"Oh, I see. I am sorry."

Gaule nodded and rubbed his tired eyes.

"A special letter." Daniel walked over and dropped an envelope on Gaule's desk. "Looks like it's your friend."

Gaule noted the sarcasm in Daniel's voice. He looked at the letter, bordered in black ink. "Matthew has always been one for theatrics. A lot of people might still be alive if he learned some humility."

"Speaking of humility." Daniel sat down and kept his voice low. "They are talking, you know."

"Who's 'they,' exactly? Anyone I care about?"

Daniel shrugged. "Everyone, I guess."

"And what are they talking about? Any*thing* I care about?"

"They claim you are no longer a man of faith," Daniel sighed. "That you no longer truly believe in the church."

"Um, I'm here, aren't I?"

"Yes, but—"

"People are dangerous, Daniel. Stupid, even. Dangerous *because* they're stupid," Gaule scoffed. Lately, fellow clergymen had begun doubting Gaule's commitment to God, and to religion in general. Gaule had been an outspoken opponent of the "witch hunting" movement that had spread across East Anglia, believing them to be a sham that spat in the face of the very God they claimed to defend. He and Matthew Hopkins, the self-appointed Witchfinder

General, had already established a short but colorful history. In fact, after following Hopkins for several months two years ago, Gaule had written a pamphlet that he had paid to have distributed. The pamphlet openly mocked Matthew Hopkins and his brutally unfair practices.

"I have not lost my faith, Daniel," Gaule said. "But I am also not stupid enough to follow it through the darkness. There is no more dangerous combination than that of ego and ignorance. I'm afraid that too many in our church have downed that toxic cocktail, and I fear what it will make of our faith. *Faith*, Daniel, whether you *believe* it or not, should be used as an agent of *good*, not one of chaos, not one of evil."

"The child…"

"Yes, *exactly*. The child. Whether I truly *believe* that there is a world beyond this one, one that's full of puppies and flowers and sunshine and rainbows, isn't relevant. But in that *moment*, in that tiny slice of time where that poor girl teetered on the edge of life, she *needed* to believe. *That* is what faith gives the world, Daniel. When you begin taking things too literally and too far, you end up with psychopaths like

Hopkins and the blood of innocent people soaking our fields."

Gaule wiped his forehead. The summer heat had taken its toll on his aging body. "Unfortunately," he continued, "people like Hopkins have weaponized our faith. Profiting off fears amidst this stupid war. Blood is being spilled over bells and incense. The world needs faith now more than ever. More importantly, it needs to believe in the *good* of faith."

The English Civil War that had been ravaging the country was sparked by King Charles' marriage to a French Catholic woman. As a result, he was slowly invoking Catholic traditions in churches—like bells and incense. This pettiness is what the English were fighting over. Differences in how to worship the same God were what was tearing the country apart and instilling fear in the masses.

"Sometimes, Daniel, the *truth* is not as important as what we *need* to believe. For the sake of our own comfort. But make no mistake when it comes to faith. If God meant for us to follow it blindly, he would not have given us eyes."

"I suppose," Daniel sighed. "I just hope you're not concerned with breaking from traditions, or what fellow clergymen think of you."

"Two things." Gaule held up two fingers. "One, I don't give a damn what fellow clergymen think of me. These are the same men who truly believe that drinking wine is literally the same thing as drinking the blood of Christ. Two...*fuck* tradition. Sometimes the past needs to die. Especially if it promotes ideas that are outright dangerous."

"Right." Daniel nodded. "I hope one day I can share your perspective, Minister Gaule."

"I hope for the sake of your own sanity that you don't have to go through what I went through to reach this perspective, Daniel." Gaule sighed and ripped open the black-bordered envelope, reading the letter from Hopkins.

The last words, on the bottom of the page, made his blood suddenly run cold.

-3-

DEMONOLOGY

JANUARY 1630

Saint John's Church in the village of Great Wenham was a charming little building featuring a single two-story tower. The brick from which it was constructed was beige, with a red roof, giving it the illusion that it may have been the child of Spanish architecture. At this time in 1630, the church's vicar was a man by the name of James Hopkins. James was a father to six boys. And every evening, they'd gather around the fire and he'd read passages from the Bible to his sons in the hopes that they'd absorb the very messages that he'd spent his life preaching.

James had begun to grow weary as his sons aged. They no longer paid much attention to his nightly sermons. They were more interested in whispering about girls or joining the military. Truly, the old ways were dying. James often found himself unfathomably saddened to know that his world, the Puritan world, was crumbling around him. The world he had grown up protecting was vanishing before his very eyes, with but a few noble souls left on Earth willing to defend it.

Luckily, one of those souls was his fourth son, 11-year-old Matthew Hopkins. Or at least he would be in time.

Matthew had been very different from his brothers. While James's other sons rebelled, Matthew remained staunchly supportive of his father. He idolized the man and hung on to every word as if they were being spoken by God Himself.

It was on this chilly night in January that James Hopkins had made a decision that, while seemingly trivial at the time, would go on to affect the course of history.

After the sermon had ended, and after James had realized that all but one of his sons was actually paying attention, he called young Matthew Hopkins into his study. The boy was scared at first. James was a strict disciplinarian and a perfectionist...a combination that resulted in more than one painful smack across Matthew Hopkins' face in his young life. Moral absolutism; that right and wrong existed in a state of black and white, was James Hopkins' philosophy. And it was one he strongly guarded, at times excessively.

James Hopkins closed the door to his study and ordered his son to sit down while he sifted through some books. Matthew did as he was told, looking nervously around the room, wondering what he did wrong. At that moment, every minor transgression he could think of raced through his mind; had he been a minute late to supper, had he not annunciated his prayers properly, had he not said grace to his father's liking? The possibilities hung heavy in his head as his father fished out an old book with a weathered cover.

James placed the book on his desk in front of his son. It was a heavy book that landed with a thud. It must have been of great importance.

Matthew looked down at the cover. Embossed on the front was a symbol he'd never before seen. It looked similar to a cross, but was fatter and more ornate. He read the book's title: *Daemonologie, In Forme of a Dialogue.*

"I don't understand," Matthew said. The boy was as confused as he was nervous. "Father, have I done wrong?"

"No." James lit a tobacco pipe. "Quite the opposite, actually." He sat down at his desk, right across from his young son, and let a long, billowing cloud of smoke out from between his lips. "Matthew," he said, "I have six sons. And only one shows any interest in continuing my work."

"I have interest!" the preteen Matthew Hopkins exclaimed. "I swear, father! I listen to everything!"

"You *were* the son I was speaking of, Matthew," his father assured him, accompanied by the throaty, amused chuckle of an Olympian god. "You must have more confidence in yourself, son. You have learned much, and, arguably, displayed the most. That is why I have brought you here tonight."

Matthew Hopkins slumped back into his chair. "Father, this book. I don't understand."

"It is an important guide, Matthew." James tapped

the book's worn leather surface. "Our world is being…invaded. And torn apart at her seams."

"By who?"

"The Devil, of course."

Matthew Hopkins should have known. He shook his head. It was *always* the Devil. What did he have against Earth, anyway?

"You see, the world is changing. For the worse. And I know why." It is easy to look back and picture James Hopkins as but a senile old man, influenced by delusion. While a zealot, he was not a bad man. He was a man driven by his own convictions, his unbreakable belief in his faith. As well as a belief in a master plan, the wheels of which he was setting in motion.

"Why?" young Matthew Hopkins asked.

"The Devil has infiltrated our world. Let me tell you, Matthew, when I was your age, the world was a better place. The crops grew thick. Disease kept its distance. And the winter offered but a cool relief from the summer heat in lieu of the harsh blizzards it throws at us now. The world was different then. It was better."

"But...why?" Matthew Hopkins was genuinely curious. "Why did things change?"

"The *world* changed," James Hopkins said. "Harlotry has become the norm. Adultery is not uncommon. Sinning...it's become not a thing spoken of in hush tones, but a thing on display all hours of the day. We have become numb to it, I'm afraid. The very things God forbids have become common practice. It is an insult to our Lord, Matthew."

Matthew nodded, understanding. "The abundance of sinning...it's why the world has gotten more frightening? More dangerous?"

"Precisely!" James Hopkins slapped his knee and took a puff of his pipe. "God is not happy, Matthew. We have allowed those of poor nature to overtake His domain. We cannot allow this any longer. And it starts here." He opened the first page of the old book. "This is a guide to cleansing the world of these monsters, Matthew. These monsters...they act as agents of the Devil. And they sully our world. We cannot have that any longer. We *must* fight back. My son, you are the only one I have who I truly feel has the strength…no…the *courage* to do what must be done. I ask you, sincerely," James Hopkins looked deep into the eyes of his young son. "Do you have that courage?"

Matthew Hopkins, but a child, took a deep breath. He puffed out his chest. "Yes, I do, father. I have the courage. To do what must be done. To do what is right. I will not let the Devil win, father."

"No matter the cost?"

"Yes."

James Hopkins leaned in. "Matthew, listen to me very carefully."

His son nodded.

And listened.

"It is easy to give your life to a cause," James said. "But it is much more difficult to give…your *soul*. Do you understand?"

Matthew Hopkins did not. But he nodded anyway. The young boy had one thing, and one thing only, in mind: pleasing his father. That was all that had ever mattered to the boy. And here he was, on the cusp of achieving the ultimate triumph over his five brothers.

"There are times where the only way to truly eliminate evil," James said, "is to do something that you may feel is evil in itself. It is an unfortunate burden laid upon us. History will not be kind to us. But this is a sacrifice we must accept."

"I understand, father."

"Good. Here." James slid the book closer to his son, who picked it up and looked over the cover. "Read this. Study it. Treat it as...a bible."

And that he would. For, you see, *Daemonologie* was no average book. In fact, it was actually a guide for how to deal with a number of supernatural creatures. From ghosts, to werewolves, to vampires, to yes, even...witches. The book outlined the techniques one might find successful when fighting against such creatures. While that may sound akin to fantasy to you or I, one must make note that this book was *literally* a Bible to young Matthew Hopkins.

The reason, of course, being that the guide on how to deal with paranormal creatures and the Bible were authored by the same person: King James.

-4-
SWINGING SHADOWS

MARCH 1645

Colchester Castle was built in 1100 AD and stood about two stories high. Constructed of old stone, the castle was located a few miles outside the village and had begun to fall into a state of disrepair. The foundation was crumbling, having been built upon the vaults of an ancient Roman temple. Vines overtook the walls, crawling over the building like the tentacles of a sea monster. Inside, the roof leaked and bats made their homes in the rafters. On stormy nights, the sound of dripping rain pattering on the floor was deafening.

The building's keep was among the largest in the world, with floor space of over 17,000 square feet. Dotting the perimeter walls of the cavernous keep were small prison cells with portcullis gates. It was in one of these cells that the old woman, Elizabeth Clarke, lay in misery the evening of her arrest. John Stearne had escorted Elizabeth to her cell while Matthew Hopkins spoke to one of the magistrates. Here, she found a barred window and some straw on the stone floor.

"We'll be back to deal with you soon, witch," John Stearne seethed, pulling a handle and letting the portcullis door fall shut with an ominous thud.

"I'm not a witch!" Elizabeth Clarke's voice was barely a whisper, having exhausted her screams on the ride over. "I'm not a witch...I'm not...I'm not..." She collapsed. She had already been tired before the evening's ordeal began. Letting her body slump to the floor, she closed her eyes and was soon asleep.

Humming. A tune, of some kind. That's all Elizabeth Clarke could hear as she awoke, staring into the darkness, at a ceiling bathed in moonlight. Her back was cold. Her face was wet. She had no idea where she was.

"Ah, I see you've decided to join us," came a voice. It belonged to a young man sitting patiently in a wooden chair, watching over her. It belonged to Matthew Hopkins. "I thought it rude not to let you gather your strength."

"My strength?" Elizabeth sat up. She was in a prison cell. Wiping her eyes, she started to remember everything. Being shaved. Being poked and prodded. Being jailed.

For being a witch.

"Yes. You slept two hours. I would have given you another. Oh, well. I will accept it as your declaration of your eagerness to begin." Hopkins stood up and continued humming sadistic tunes as he sifted through his bag.

"Begin what?"

"The extraction of a confession, my dear," Hopkins explained cheerily. "You see, proof is no longer good enough in the eyes of most magistrates to convict one of witchcraft. A confession from the accused is more appropriate."

"You shall get no such thing!" Elizabeth Clarke spat. "You're insane if you think I'm going to admit to such a ridiculous thing! You might as well not waste your time or mine!"

"Why, Ms. Clarke, I am *insulted.*" Hopkins pulled a leather notebook from his bag. It was old and worn. The pages inside were yellowed and fraying at the edges. On the front, he had carved his initials into the leather. "As I told you before, I desire your innocence! I don't *want* you to confess!" He smiled. A fake smile. A liar's smile. "However, it is my *duty* to hold you to the highest standards and unfortunately that means subjecting you to the strictest forms of interrogation in order to ensure your innocence. I assure you, once we are satisfied and have proof of your innocence, I promise you will go free."

He showed her the cover of the leather notebook. His initials were carved in the front. "Do you see this? A long time ago, I was given a book about how to weed out witchcraft. 'Daemonologie,' it was called. Wonderful piece of literature." Hopkins smiled, remembering his many nights by the fire reading that book. "But, it has become somewhat obsolete. Out of date. So, I started my own book." He patted the journal. "With techniques on hunting witches and extracting confessions passed down for generations. This is my new Bible, Ms. Clarke. And I intend to follow it to the letter."

"What are you going to do?" Elizabeth Clarke asked. "Are you going to torture me?"

"Heavens, no! Torture is illegal." Matthew Hopkins laughed. "*Interrogation*, my dear. They're very different." He took her hand and gently kissed it, then looked deep into the old woman's eyes. "I offer you my promise that we will not inflict any physical harm on you, whatsoever."

As those with silver tongues have been known to twist and manipulate the meaning of words throughout the ages, so too did Matthew Hopkins that night. Torture was indeed illegal, but it was relegated to direct physical harm. Matthew Hopkins' method was what he deemed interrogation, though the line between the two is thin and blurry.

Elizabeth Clarke was subjected to four days of sleep deprivation. Hopkins, Stearne, or one of their female assistants would rotate in and spend time walking Elizabeth Clarke back and forth through the halls of Colchester Castle. Every time she collapsed, whoever was watching her picked her up and made her keep walking. By the middle of the fourth night, Clarke was hallucinating, teetering between the real world and the dream world.

Hopkins recognized this. He saw her glazed-over eyes and heard her slurred speech. She was as good as drunk. Sensing his chance, Hopkins sat Elizabeth down at a bench in the hall and spoke in a warm, kind voice. "Ms. Clarke, I hate seeing you like this. You can end this with a confession."

"I...shall...not..." her voice was weak and raspy. Her breaths short and shallow.

"My dear," Hopkins lowered his voice. "I understand you are afraid. What if I could offer you safety, despite a confession? Perhaps if you cooperated with something, I could offer you safe passage through the legal system."

Elizabeth Clarke looked up with wide eyes.

"I know you fear the gallows. I can spare you from them. But only if you cooperate. And confess. Think of it as a plea bargain."

"I will," Clarke finally said. "I will."

"Good. First, I need you to sign this confession."

Hopkins handed her a slip of parchment with a written confession. Clarke eagerly signed the bottom, feeling the weight of her exhaustion lift off her shoulders. "Next," Hopkins said, ripping a blank page from his leather notebook, "I need you to do something for me."

"Anything..."

"Give me names."

Elizabeth Clarke named 19 women who she believed could have possibly been witches. Truthfully, she simply named everyone she knew, hoping each name would increase the chances of her avoiding the gallows.

The women had slowly been brought to Colchester Castle over the following days. Each one screamed and pleaded. Elizabeth's heart sank as she watched each accused witch be dragged across the stone floor and thrown into a cage.

Among the women were young Rebecca West and her mother, Anne West. Rebecca, unlike her mother, was calm as she was arrested. While her mother struggled in the arms of Hopkins' assistants, Rebecca calmly walked with a confident happiness to her steps. She smiled and waved at Elizabeth Clarke as she was escorted past her cell.

The girl knows, Clarke thought. *She knows I pointed fingers.* Truthfully, Clarke thought none of the women were witches. But she was tired, and desperate. Now, the guilt had begun to build in the pit of her stomach. For she knew, in the back of her mind, that many of these women would soon be dead because of her.

That night, after the last accused witch had been imprisoned, the castle lay silent but for the faint weeping of the women awaiting their fates, wondering why God would betray them.

However, sometime around midnight, a gentle singing reverberated through the castle's stone walls: "*My own fairest daughter, your bride shall be. If you will swim alongside, our enemies. And send them to the depths, of the Lowland Sea.*"

"*Stop!*" shouted John Stearne as he banged on the portcullis of Rebecca West's cell. "The singing's making me head throb!"

"It was that bad, was it?" Rebecca West tapped her chin. "Perhaps you just have poor taste in music."

"Rebecca!" her mother whispered from the cell next to her. "Stop! Show some respect!"

"Listen to your mother, girl," John Stearne said. "And you just might survive this."

"Hmm," Rebecca playfully crossed her arms and smiled. "I have a greater concern."

John Stearne squinted through the metal gate at the girl's defiant form. "And what would that concern be?"

"That you might not survive this."

John Stearne's body went cold. He suddenly felt light-headed. Then he heard a squeak and felt something running up his leg.

A rat!

He felt the vermin pawing at his legs. "Get if off!" He danced about, shaking his leg until the rat finally escaped and darted between the grating of Rebecca's cell, into her waiting hands. It climbed up her shoulder and nuzzled her neck.

"Filth!" Stearne barked through the prison cell.

"I assure you," Rebecca West said, "that his fur is much cleaner than your soul."

Three weeks passed. Elizabeth Clarke and the women she had accused had been confined within the walls of Colchester Castle. They had been given more company over the past few days as more and more women named other potential witches in the village in the hopes of having their sentences reduced. There were 29 women and seven men imprisoned by the time court convened in April of 1645.

Hopkins and his team had extracted confessions from every single prisoner. The most difficult had been Anne West. The woman was a widow, and it was frequently assumed in the 17th century that any woman who outlived her husband, especially at such a young age, must have obviously made a contract with the Devil to have him killed and inherit his fortunes.

While Anne West took six nights of sleep deprivation to finally coax a confession, her daughter Rebecca *giggled* as she signed hers. The other women looked on in horror, fearing the woman had either made a deal with the witch hunters that would result in their own deaths…or that she was simply just *mad*.

On the morning the verdicts were read, most of the village had gathered in Colchester Castle. Many of them cheered on as guilty verdicts were announced by the magistrate. They truly believed that the pacts with the Devil by these men and women were the reason for their ills and misfortunes.

When it was over, 26 of the 36 accused had been condemned to hang, including Elizabeth Clarke and Anne West. When Elizabeth's name was called as among the guilty, she gave Matthew Hopkins a hurt stare of betrayal. The man did not offer a look back, instead clapping along with the rest of the crowd who wanted to see witches executed.

An hour later, the accused had been lined up behind the gallows. There were only four ropes, so four prisoners were executed at once. The process was well-oiled; four accused would come up, be read their last rites, and then hanged. Sometimes their necks snapped and they stopped moving immediately. Other times it took ten or even fifteen minutes before a body went limp and urine streamed down their legs. All of them pleaded their innocence, and each time they did, the crowd booed and condemned them, calling them liars, sinners, and blaming them for bringing on the hardships that had plagued the village.

Elizabeth Clarke and Anne West were executed in the same batch. Clarke was fairly stoic, feeling defeated and tired. She had no qualms about simply ending it at this point. A part of her was looking forward to it. She'd lived 80 years and most had been miserable. Her only regret was that she'd be remembered as a witch, as a monster, when she most certainly was not.

I suppose it is better than being forgotten.

Anne West screamed her innocence. But her protests were drowned out by the crowd, roaring for blood. "Speak to the Devil when you see him!" "Enjoy the Hell you've brought upon our village!" "You're lucky we have not decided to burn you instead, witch!"

An executioner placed a rope around Anne West's neck and tightened it until she could barely scream.

Then, with little ceremony, he kicked the woman off the gallows platform.

It was a quick death. A merciful death. The woman's neck cracked in two and her body went stiff in the breeze. The crowd applauded as her cries of terror were immediately cut off.

Next was Elizabeth Clarke's turn. She closed her eyes and said a prayer as the executioner tightened a rope around her neck as well. When she opened her eyes, she caught the dark, black spheres of Matthew Hopkins' eyes staring back at her. He was at the back of the crowd, standing proudly with his arms crossed. He looked on with a sinister smile.

Elizabeth felt a boot kick her back and she was pushed off the platform and into the abyss. Unlike Anne West, her death was neither quick nor merciful. The old woman twisted and curled in the air as she hung by her neck. Her face turned blue and she gurgled, her eyes bugging from her head as her leg kicked back and forth. The prosthetic fell off, landing in the mud below. Finally, after several minutes, Elizabeth Clarke, the first woman persecuted by Matthew Hopkins, was dead. Her body swung stiffly in the breeze, the shadow of her fresh corpse swaying over the crowd.

As the last witch was hanged and the crowd dispersed, Matthew Hopkins collected his payment from the magistrate. Afterwards, he walked back to his cart, where John Stearne was tending to the horses.

"How much this time?" Stearne asked.

Matthew Hopkins tossed him the sack of coins. "One pound per witch. Enough to keep us in business for quite some time."

From behind the witch hunters' cart, there was a familiar voice: "One pound? Is that it?"

Rebecca West emerged. She had been spared the gallows by the magistrate, though Matthew Hopkins did not know how. He suspected that her age was a factor. Perhaps their weak wills drew the line at executing teenagers, despite the danger he knew harlots like Rebecca West brought to their villages. They were easy targets for the Devil because their minds were already so corrupt.

"What do you want?" Hopkins asked with an angry, spiteful snarl.

"Well, I'm a tad perturbed, if you want honesty,"

Rebecca said. "I was quite fond of my mother, you know. After my father's death, she would rock me to sleep at night. I'm not certain what I'll do now, on my own."

"Then maybe you and your whore mother should have thought of that before making a deal with sin," Hopkins fumed. "I do not know how you escaped conviction, but I promise that my work here is not done. Watch your back."

"Oh, don't worry about me," Rebecca smiled. "I pity you, you know?"

"Pity *me?* I'll remember that," Matthew leapt up into the driver's seat of the carriage. "I shall take comfort in your pity as I am enjoying my fancy meal that I purchased with the blood of your mother."

"If you're looking for me to lash out," Rebecca said calmly, "you're wasting your time. I should warn you, Mr. Hopkins, that you cannot make me angry. I have grown far beyond retaliation for petty insults from people who feel the need to make them. But I do pity you. Very much so, in point of fact. I pity you because you are blind."

"Am I?" Hopkins was getting both frustrated and uncomfortable. He looked at Stearne, "John, let's go. There are other towns and other witches." The two men took off down the road in the carriage, their female companions in the back. Behind them, Rebecca West stared, her form growing smaller and smaller as they got farther away, finally leaving the village far behind.

Their reign of terror, however, was just beginning.

-5-

ASHES AND DARKNESS

FEBRUARY 1644

ONE YEAR BEFORE THE ARREST OF ELIZABETH CLARKE

Fire. An elemental monster responsible for both creation and destruction. It is fire that welds the swords of a battle, the glasses and potteries and stones that make up the walls of fortresses and keeps. But it has a dark side. It also consumed the very things it once formed.

St. Andrews Church in Cambridgeshire had stood for hundreds of years. But on this night, the once-beautiful stone house of worship was engulfed in flames. Like a dying beast, the building collapsed in on itself, wood and glass splintering in all directions.

From their horses, William Dowsing and his team of iconoclasts watched until they were satisfied that the church was but hours from being a pile of ashes in the snow. A monument that stood for centuries reduced to a pile of rubble. Then, they took off down the road, toward the parish of Great Wenham. Dowsing had been to two villages over the past week; Wenham would be his last stop before taking a month's hiatus, and he was looking forward to spending time with his family.

William Dowsing was a radical puritan and had been commissioned by the Earl of Manchester to travel across East Anglia and destroy any "objects of idolatry and superstition." This included many Catholic staples such as fixed altars, crucifixes, crosses, and even certain stained glass windows. There were times where a church was so decorated with Catholic regalia that it was easier to simply burn the building down, as they had just done with St. Andrews. It has been estimated that Dowsing either partially or completely destroyed around 250 churches over his two-year career.

Hours after destroying St. Andrews, Dowsing and his team arrived in the village of Great Wenham, a quaint little town near the confluence of two large rivers. Ordering the rest of his men to find an inn and rent some rooms, Dowsing went to visit St. Johns Church, which served as the home of the Hopkins family.

In the chilly night, Dowsing knocked on the front door of the church. There was no answer at first, so he pounded. He knew someone was inside.

Finally, the door was opened, and Dowsing was greeted by the tall, lanky form of John Hopkins. John was two years older than his younger brother, Matthew. But unlike Matthew, he had become the minister of the church...much to his own dismay. The truth was that John Hopkins was planning on leaving soon to pursue other careers, though historians now agree that he was actually removed before he could leave voluntarily.

"Can I help you?" John asked Dowsing.

"You know why I'm here."

John sighed. "I do. And I assure you, William, that there is nothing here left to 'reform,' as the Earl has so elegantly put it."

"I figured as much." William Dowsing nodded. "I see you have carried on your father's will. May I come in?"

Minutes later, William Dowsing and John Hopkins were in the church's administrative office. Hopkins poured Dowsing a glass of white wine. "It's been years, uncle," John Hopkins said. "I hear you've been busy."

William Dowsing and James Hopkins had been good friends in their youth. The two were both staunch puritans with the same fear that the world was changing for the worse, and that aggression was the only way to stop it. But whereas James became a vicar, Dowsing had become a soldier.

"I have been busy." Dowsing nodded.

"Destroying churches across England?"

"Destroying heresy, John." Dowsing sipped the wine. It was the best he'd had in quite some time. "The old ways, the *good* ways, they're dying."

"And you believe the only way to save them is to destroy the new ones?"

Dowsing shrugged. "More or less."

"And you see no irony in this? Destruction is a trait of the Devil, of evil, is it not?"

"I will admit it is not easy," Dowsing said. "But for

one to truly complete the work of God, one must be willing to what must be done."

"At any cost to your soul." John shook his head and poured his own glass of wine. He sat back at his desk and sighed. "Have you been to Manningtree?"

"No. Why?"

"Matthew moved there, years ago. When my father passed away, we each received an inheritance. Generous ones, I might add. Though none as much as Matthew's."

"Jealous, are you?"

"Perhaps. Though it makes sense. Matthew was always father's favorite."

"He's a *believer*," Dowsing said. "As am I, and as was your father. Or at least he used to be."

"Oh, he's still a believer, that's for sure," John ensured him. "He still hasn't married. No woman is 'pure' enough for him. Please." John rolled his eyes. "Any woman who doesn't immediately throw up when she looks at me is pure enough for me."

"You said he lives in Manningtree, now?"

"Yes. When my father died, he took it very hard.

He didn't speak for days. He was convinced that he was killed by someone who had made a pact with the Devil because of his commitment to God. He believed that, because my father had been preaching so furiously against witchcraft, that a witch decided to take him out and shut him up, so to speak."

"And what do you think?" It was obvious that Dowsing was not totally convinced it *wasn't* a witch.

"Fantasy," John said. "My father was old and sick. He was going to die, witch or no witch. That is the reality that I fear many people cannot accept."

"Perhaps people just refuse to believe in coincidence, John."

"A coincidence implies suspicious timing. My father was eighty years old. His time was long passed."

Dowsing grinned. "I won't argue with you, John. I simply wanted to stop by and see you. It's been too long."

"Agreed. A toast to health. And hopefully a swift end to this war that has claimed too many lives."

The two drank beneath the flicker of torchlight.

Outside, they could hear the crunching of snow as horses marched by. They spoke of the war, and of John's lack of commitment to the church. John Hopkins had made it no secret that he was here because it paid. Not that he didn't believe in God, of course. But he did not consider himself a puritan nor a Catholic. He preferred Anglicanism, the middle way, but this was often seen as a cop-out as opposed to the all-or-nothing, for-us-or-against-us approach many others took.

"When is the last time," Dowsing finally asked as they finished the bottle of wine, "that you saw Matthew?"

"Five years ago, he passed by. Said he'd purchased an inn in Manningtree, the Thorn Inn. He seemed...odd. His hair was long and unkempt. He'd put on weight. His beard was gray. He was only, God, twenty-three years old the last time I saw him? But he already looked as weathered as a middle-aged man."

"Perhaps it is the stress of these disastrous winters. And the emotional toll of losing his father. I have lost people. It does things to your mind, and your body, that one might mistake for old age."

"Not like this," John Hopkins said. "The last thing I did was wish him luck in his travels." He stared into space as he spoke. The memory had obviously left quite an impression. "He told me that he did not need luck when he had the backing of God. He truly believes that he is a warrior for the light, but...when I looked in my brother's eyes, I saw something else."

"What did you see, John?"

"Darkness. Pure, darkness."

-6-
WAILS AND FALLS

MARCH 1645

Wailing. Horrible, ghostly wailing. It penetrated the walls of Elizabeth Clarke's home and echoed off the floors and ceilings. She couldn't sleep. She couldn't think. The screaming, the crying, the bawling; it went on night after night, and even scared away her feline companions. It drove her mad.

One night in March 1645, Clarke had decided that enough was enough. She threw a blanket over her shoulders and lumbered outside into the cold. The house next to her, separated by only a few feet, seemed to be the source of the arrant sobbing that had kept her awake going on several nights. She couldn't take it anymore.

Elizabeth Clarke pounded on the door of the Rivet house. John Rivet, the local tailor, answered the door and the screaming got even louder, piercing Clarke's ears.

"Your child!" Elizabeth Clarke complained. "Does it have a lever to turn it off or is someone going to have to smack it upside the head?"

"How dare you!" John Rivet growled back. "It is a *child*. Children cry. Perhaps you even were one once!"

"Trust me, if I was a child like that then I would have been grateful to my parents for smothering me with a pillow till my heart stopped beating, thus sparing the world from such ungodly noise!"

John Rivet wasn't going to take such abuse from the old hag. "Good*night*, Ms. Clarke." He slammed the door in her face.

She knocked a few more times, but Rivet ignored it and went to the bedroom, where his wife slept soundly. She'd gotten used to their infant son's cries. Most of the village had, he suspected, since Elizabeth Clarke was the only one to grumble. At least openly. While he was sure his child's nightly cries kept others awake, they were at least decent enough neighbors to understand that there was nothing he could do!

His infant son, Edward, had fussed much more than the other babies born in the village throughout the years. The local physicians suspected that he may have suffered from night terrors, causing him to scream through all hours of the night. John Rivet, while conscious of the baby's wails, also knew that there was little he could do to stop them. Thus, he and his wife had just grown accustomed. Hopefully the cries would stop soon enough. Lord knows he might eventually have *everyone* on Elizabeth Clarke's side if they didn't.

John Rivet crawled into bed with his wife and fell asleep to his son's cries, a process to which he was now well-acclimated. When he awoke the next morning, the cries had stopped. This, again, had become common practice. The child's screams typically faded as the night went on and he fell into a deeper sleep.

John went to check on his son when he noticed he wasn't breathing in his crib. This momentary flash of disbelief was followed by panic as he ripped the baby from its crib and shook it, hoping to wake the child.

Instead, the baby boy hung limp in his father's arms, his eyes rolled to the back of his head and his skin had turned pale blue.

"No!" John Rivet shouted in agony, waking his wife, who joined in the mourning the moment she saw the corpse of her infant son dangling before her like the lifeless husks of rabbit or pheasant she'd purchase at the markets.

When it was clear the child was dead, John Rivet placed the body on the floor of his house and prayed, wiping the tears from his eyes as he spoke. He lifted the baby's shirt, exposing its stomach, where he found something peculiar: a mark. It appeared to be a raised, red bump under the skin, right above the child's belly button. It was in the shape of a twinkling star, like an asterisk. When John realized what it was, and while his wife was still bawling in the corner, he felt a rage surge through his body like lightning.

"A witch…" he said, gritting his teeth. He flipped the kitchen table over, spilling food onto the floor. "A witch!"

"What witch, John?" Mrs. Rivet asked through tears, her face flustered and hair matted.

John Rivet looked at the door. It was more than obvious who had done this. Only one word came to mind: "Clarke."

John Rivet wanted to confront the old woman head on. His blood boiled so hard that he was ready to end the miserable old hag's life all by himself. It was his wife that stopped him, urging him to go to the local magistrate instead. She reminded him that he was all she had left, and him going to prison for murder would leave her with nothing.

So John Rivet spoke to the local magistrate. It was clear he was angry, shouting at the old man behind the counter, "Elizabeth Clarke killed my son!"

The clerk looked startled. "That's…uh…that's quite an accusation. Do you have any proof of this?"

"I…no…but…"

"Then from where does this accusation come?" The clerk adjusted his glasses without even bothering to look up at John Rivet, instead preferring to jot down mindless notes.

"My child is…was…" he gulped, suppressing the sadness that had otherwise been hidden behind a veil of anger. "…my child was a bit loud. She complained.

Last night, she complained that my son was being too noisy. This morning my son was dead. It is not coincidence."

The magistrate looked uninterested.

Then, perhaps out of certainty that Elizabeth Clarke was the killer of his son, or perhaps out of frustration and grief, John Rivet told a lie. A lie that would have a ripple effect through all of English history.

"She said," John Rivet explained, "that she'd have me smother my son beneath a pillow, lest she'd kill him herself."

The magistrate looked up. Suddenly, he was curious. "So, she made a direct threat?"

"Yes," Rivet lied. "She told me she would kill my son. And she made good on her promise. Her pact."

"And was he smothered?"

"No." Rivet lowered his voice and leaned in. "This morning, I found a mark on my son's corpse. It was red. Like the eyes of the Devil. A mark like the twinkle of a star. An insidious mark if I've ever seen one. I believe that Ms. Clarke is a witch. She made a pact with the Devil to take my son because she had grown frustrated with his cries. I promise you this is the truth. She must be punished."

The magistrate stroked his chin. "Accusations of witchcraft are very serious, Mr. Rivet. It is an executable offense."

"She would deserve nothing less," Rivet replied sternly. "She took my son's life. She does not deserve her own after such evil."

"Be that as it may," the magistrate coughed, "I cannot authorize an investigation without—"

Just then, there was commotion outside. A young man came through the doors, out of breath from apparently running in a panic. He looked at the magistrate clerk. "Sir…horses…dead…"

"Calm down," the clerk said. "What's the problem, son?"

"Two horses just dropped dead out of nowhere, sir. We've no clue as to why. S'as if they just had their life sapped. We suspect witchcraft, sir."

The magistrate exchanged knowing looks with John Rivet. He then addressed the boy again. "Young man, where are these dead horses?"

"They fell dead right in front of a house, sir."

"Which house?"

"Why," the boy said, "the house of Elizabeth Clarke, the old crone."

John Rivet eyed the clerk. "Still believe in coincidence?"

The clerk sighed. Even a skeptic, could no longer doubt the obvious. "You're in luck. A team of supposed witch hunters have taken up rooms at the inn. A Mr. Matthew Hopkins and his associate, John Stearne. From Manningtree."

"Witch hunters, you say?"

"Supposedly. Matthew Hopkins even has a title from parliament, the Witchfinder General. If anyone can determine if Ms. Clarke is truly a witch, it's them. In any case, do not fret, Mr. Rivet. Mourn your loss, for which I am sorry. But justice, I assure you, will be served."

Witchfinder General was indeed the title that Matthew Hopkins so graciously went by. However, it was not assigned from parliament. In fact parliament, at this point in time, did not know that Matthew Hopkins even existed.

During the English Civil War, there was a three-year period where the government was, for lack of a better term, closed. There were few formal courts as the government had focused on the war effort; taxation, for example, being a new revenue stream that needed overseeing. As such, many local parishes were free to hold their own courts with their own magistrates. Though, just as Matthew Hopkins had made up his "official" government title, the trials at the time were little more than fraudulent kangaroo courts meant to weed out witches...or anyone else who posed a problem.

A problem like Elizabeth Clarke.

The witch hunt, it seemed, had officially begun.

-7-
BLINDNESS

MAY 1645

It was raining in the village. Hard. The muddy roads quickly filled with mucky water. The straw roofs leaked like mad. The cattle took shelter and the chickens fluttered their wet feathers about. As lightning crackled in the distance, a man on a lone horse arrived in town. His horse slopped through the mud before stopping in front of the local magistrate's office.

When the man dismounted and removed his hood, it became clear to the townsfolk that he was not wearing a cloak, but the robes of a clergyman. The man walked inside, his robes dripping wet, and spoke to the surprised clerk behind the counter. "I need to know the location of the house of Elizabeth Clarke."

"And, um, who exactly are you?"

"John Gaule, vicar of Great Staughton."

The clerk's eyes went wide. Clergymen were treated like royalty in 17th-century England, and John Gaule was no exception. "I apologize, vicar Gaule. Elizabeth Clarke's home is now county property."

"Correct, and I am a representative of a neighboring county here to investigate a potential threat. Article eight, section two outlines this very clearly, that neighboring counties shall not impede an investigation that could possibly affect the safety of said neighboring county."

The clerk shook his head in confusion. In truth, he'd never heard of that article...or even had any idea what John Gaule was talking about...but he couldn't let the vicar know that.

"Ah...I understand," the clerk said sheepishly. "Ms. Clarke's home is on the third street from the north, painted with an X on the front door."

"Thank you. Now, that wasn't too difficult, was it?"

The clerk glared. Royalty or not, he was not a fan of being patronized. "No, I suppose it wasn't. Will there be anything *else* today?"

"Yes," Gaule said. "I'd like a list prepared of all of the people executed last week. I would like to speak to the families."

"But—"

"Ah, ah, ah." Gaule wagged his finger. "Article eight, section two…"

The clerk grunted. "Be right back." Then he disappeared down the hall to retrieve the list.

John Gaule easily found the former home of Elizabeth Clarke. True to the clerk's word, a white X had been painted on the door, perhaps as a warning to any potential squatters that the house was now property of the county. Gaule still couldn't believe the clerk bought his lie; he'd simply made up a rule on the spot hoping that the magistrate had little familiarity with them. It worked almost *too* well. *Worryingly* well. *Why do county magistrates not know their own rules?*

The door was unlocked and John Gaule made his

way inside. It was dark and humid. Nesting bugs scurried beneath the walls as light flooded inside when he opened the door.

Inside, Gaule pulled back the curtain on the home's lone window, letting in even more light. He poked around for several minutes. He examined Clarke's desk, where she'd collected half-legible letters and nothing more. Certainly nothing suspicious. He looked under her bed, in her dresser, anywhere he might find a clue as to how Matthew Hopkins' arrest of her truly played out. He had made himself familiar with the case, or at least the stories of the case. But he wanted to see things for himself.

That's when he saw something glinting in the sunlight. Gaule leaned down near the front of the fireplace, where, beneath a chair, was a long, rusted razorblade. He picked it up held it close.

"You son of a bitch," Gaule whispered, shaking his head. *You used torture to get a confession.*

John Gaule was very aware that the only way to convict was with a confession. It was believed, at the time, that evidence was not enough. It was a confession or often nothing. The problem, though, was that to get around this little hurdle, magistrates and their enforcers would go to *great* lengths to extract them, often crossing ethical boundaries to do so.

As he examined the razorblade, a stray cat brushed against his leg. Gaule pat it on the head. "You must be one of Clarke's 'Familiars.' Hmph. You're awfully cute for a demon." He scratched the animal under the neck. "So, which one are you?" Carefully, he picked up the cat, sat in the chair in front of the fireplace, and set the animal on his lap, where he stroked its back as it purred.

Gaule stared ahead from the chair where Elizabeth Clarke had been constrained the night she was arrested. Directly in front of him was Clarke's countertop where she kept her food and spices and other ingredients. And the first thing he saw was a mason jar, "vinegar" written on its label.

Gaule chuckled and looked down at the cat. "So, I wonder if you're Vinegar Tom."

"Is that what you're naming him?" came a soft, feminine voice from the doorframe. "That's not very creative, if you ask me. He's already a cat who has to eat mice, at least give him something more beastly."

Gaule squinted at the young girl leaning against the door. "Who are you?"

"Rebecca. Rebecca West." She walked into the home and looked around. "I haven't been here in months. In fact, not since the night she was arrested. I was here, you know."

Gaule shook his head, confused. He found something odd about this encounter. Certainly, after investigating the homes of dozens of executed 'witches,' this was the first time his work had been interrupted by a teenage girl.

"Excuse me," Gaule raised his hand, "you...you were *here* the night she was arrested?"

"Well, I wasn't here *when* she was arrested. Right before it. My mother asked me to borrow flour from Ms. Clarke. I didn't want to. She was quite crotchety. Quite mad. But, I did love my mother. Pity." She sighed and sat on the bed, bouncing on the straw. She suddenly looked melancholy as she kicked at the dirt with her bare feet.

"Wait," Gaule found himself recalling the names of those executed the week prior, "Rebecca West...you were accused. And your mother..." He got quiet as the realization struck him. "I'm sorry. I'm sure Anne was a good woman."

"A weak one," Rebecca said. "But a good one."

"Right." Gaule stood, traipsing about the home, picking up random objects then setting them back down. He had trouble speaking without moving. Always had. He had been known to give his sermons while pacing back and forth and making wild hand gestures. "Would you like me to say a prayer, child?"

Rebecca laughed. "No thanks, 'child,'" she mocked. "I apologize, but God and I have what you might call a 'strained' relationship. If you wish to pray, I would not protest. But don't do it on my behalf."

"Ah," Gaule smiled, "I can see immediately why you labeled your mother as a weak woman. Perhaps all are, when compared to you."

Rebecca West shrugged. "You can say that about most things regarding me."

"Even arrogance?"

"If the shoe fits." She winked.

This is a smart kid, Gaule thought.

"So, Rebecca, how exactly did you escape the gallows?"

"These." She squeezed her breasts together.

Gaule raised his eyebrows.

"I persuaded one of the magistrates to ensure I was not convicted. I was raised believing that *all* talents should be used, Mr. Gaule."

"So, you know who I am," Gaule smiled triumphantly. "You overheard me at the magistrate's office. And then you followed me here. Now, Rebecca, I can only assume that your personal interest in this case has to do with vengeance for your mother."

"You could say that. While I cannot say I loved her, I can say I was fond of her. I can also say that she did not deserve her fate. She was not so much a witch as a saint."

"So, we are on the same side."

"Perhaps." Rebecca stood. "What are you doing here, Mr. Gaule?"

"Looking for evidence that this 'witch hunter,' Matthew Hopkins, has had innocent people executed." He looked through her pantry.

"What kind of evidence?"

"Oh, like that she was tortured into confession."

"But the Rivet child died right after she said she wanted it to," Rebecca reminded him. "Then they found a Devil's Mark. And she even named her Familiars!"

"Ah, yes." Gaule walked over to the rack of spices. "Names like Vinegar Tom." He showed Rebecca the jar of vinegar. "Sack and Sugar." He pointed to a sack of sugar on the counter, which would have been directly in Clarke's view as she was being tortured. "Jamara." In the window sill was plant box. Brown grass was growing out of the soil. This was Jamara, a plant from India that was said to emit oils that brought about relaxation. It wasn't uncommon for people to keep it in their homes.

"Clever," Rebecca West said. "And the last one? Holt?"

Gaule crossed his arms. "Clarke was a widow. The widow of Holt Clarke."

"Interesting…"

"It would appear that Ms. Elizabeth Clarke made

everything up under duress. Undoubtedly duress spurred on by this." He held up the razorblade.

"Alright...who are you?" Rebecca asked. "Are you a detective?"

"A vicar, actually."

"And that means what, to me?"

"I oversee the religious community of a small city some kilometers away."

"So, you're a minister?"

"More or less."

"Who dapples in finding witches..."

"I have more interest in finding the people who claim to find witches. Because I believe they knowingly execute innocent people."

"You're a...a hunter of witch hunters. A witch hunter hunter." She nodded in approval. "I like it. Does that mean you do not believe in witchcraft? Despite the things people have said they've seen?"

Gaule chuckled, glancing at the girl. She seemed genuinely interested in the subject. Rebecca West had been raised in a world where scientific discoveries were beginning to become indistinguishable from sorcery. Yet, incredibly, the superstitions of the past still remained firmly ingrained in society.

"What's so funny?" Rebecca West asked.

"Stand back a moment."

"Excuse me?"

"Please, humor me." He motioned for her to take a few steps backward. She reluctantly did, though she made her suspicion clear with her facial expression.

When there was a good amount of space between them, Gaule put his hands in his pockets and pulled out what appeared to be two silk bags of pebbles. He took two small handfuls of these pebbles and then *hurled* them at the ground as hard as he could, where they erupted in a green flame that *popped* and sparkled into vibrant reds and yellows. The spectacle lasted only a moment before it was gone, the colors fading into embers that died on the floor.

"What on *Earth* was that?!" Rebecca's eyes were wide. "Was that magic?! *Real* magic?!"

"Not the slightest," remarked Gaule. "It was simply a trick of fire. Chemicals in the stones reacted in such a way to produce colors of light. The Chinese used these fire tricks a thousand years ago to ward away evil spirits. Now they are used to create illusions."

"Well, it looked like magic to me!"

"Magic is but a trick that science has not yet found an explanation for, Rebecca." Gaule put his hood back on and stepped outside. "There's nothing left for me here. I need to find Hopkins."

Rebecca followed him out into the rain. "Mr. Gaule, you never answered my question. Does this mean that you do not believe in witches?"

"I believe that when people are scared, when winters such as this have destroyed crops and spread sickness, that people will find someone to blame. Even if they have to make that someone up. It is an unfortunate trait of human nature that we must always find outside influences to disparage before looking within ourselves. We are, sadly, the only species on this planet to blind ourselves from the truth for the sake of our own selfishness."

Rebecca smirked. "You're a fascinating man, Mr. Gaule. You seem well-educated. I do not see a wedding ring. A bachelor?"

"You could say that's the path I've chosen. At least

now, anyway. Married twice. Divorced twice. To the same woman. I've decided that a life of solitude is a life of simplicity."

"Ha," Rebecca laughed. "So you learned your lesson the second time around?"

"You could say that." He shook water from his hood as thunder rumbled amongst the swirling gray sky. "Here is some advice, Ms. West. When someone shows you who they truly are, *believe them the first time.*"

"Wise words from a wise man."

"Words from a man who was a fool." They reached his horse and he hopped on. "I appreciate your assistance, Ms. West. I understand that Mr. Hopkins is on the road. I hope to catch him and have a little chat."

"Wait!" Rebecca pleaded. "I want to go with you. I have a horse!"

"Nonsense."

"It's not nonsense!" She ran in front of his horse, blocking it. "Hopkins killed my mother. My father's been dead for years. I don't care about any of the people in this village. These are the same ones who cheered at my mother's death. There is *nothing* left for me here. Let me travel with you. Let me help bring Hopkins what he deserves."

"Do not let vengeance poison your heart, child," Gaule said. "I can assure you from experience that it can turn you into the very monster you wish to hunt."

"It's not just for my mother!" Rebecca exclaimed. The rain grew heavier. It cascaded down her shoulders. She brushed her soaked hair out of her eyes and looked back up at Gaule. "It's for everyone who died that day. And for every person Hopkins will send to the gallows between now and whenever you bring him to justice. Perhaps that time can be shortened if you have a companion to help."

Gaule finally sighed. "You have a horse?"

"And money. I won't ask you to pay my way, I just want to ride along. Help if I can. It's all I'm asking for. Please. My life means nothing here. Maybe it can mean something out there."

After several moments of contemplation, John Gaule finally gave in. "Fine."

Shortly afterward, the pair set off through the

countryside on their horses. Racing to catch up with Matthew Hopkins before he sent more innocents to their deaths. They were, as Rebecca had put it, the witch hunter hunters. Little did they know, however, that by the time they finally reached Hopkins, his path of destruction would have already grown.

-8-
LIVING WAGES

JULY 1645

An enormous tree sat like a god in the town square of Chelmsford. The tree was centuries old with a trunk as thick as a giant's thigh. Its spindly dead branches hung low. On this cool, foggy morning, the shadows of corpses were draped across the town square. 23 women had been accused of and executed for witchcraft thanks to the efforts of Matthew Hopkins and his partner John Stearne. But instead of gallows, the magistrate had decided to execute all witches at once using excess rope and the tree in the center of the village.

It had been quite the show. Since there were only two executioners in town, a number of volunteers had been pulled from the crowd of villagers who had come to cheer on the deaths of the witches and the end of their troubles. In unison, the executioners and volunteers pulled on the ropes that lifted the 23 women to their deaths. Almost all of them went painfully and struggled as they were lifted, shortly before dying of asphyxiation.

23 women killed at once. For the crime of having convened with the Devil.

For the crime of being accused.

The weight of an accusation was so heavy that the conviction rate of accused witches was incredibly high. Even though a confession was needed to formally convict, they could in theory imprison and torture you for *life* if you *didn't* confess.

And the money, at least for Matthew Hopkins and John Stearne, was good. In fact, one town had even begun to issue a tax on its citizens just to help pay for Hopkins' services.

"Nineteen, twenty, twenty-one," the Chelmsford treasurer counted out coins to Matthew Hopkins. "Twenty-two, and twenty-three."

Hopkins eagerly bagged the coins and tipped his hat to the treasurer.

"Sir," the treasurer said before Hopkins could leave. "A word, first."

"Why, of course." Hopkins smiled. "Are you not satisfied with the scope of our work? Twenty-three accusations and twenty-three convictions. Can't do much better than that."

"No, no, that's understood," the treasurer assured him. "Actually, we are more than happy with the work you've done, Mr. Hopkins. Which is why we'd actually like to ask for another service."

Hopkins was intrigued. "Oh? I'm afraid we don't hunt vampires or werewolves, if that's what you're asking."

"No, of course not. Vampires and werewolves belong in fairytales," the treasurer said. "But we would like to ask you for something we find to be of great importance, Mr. Hopkins. And we will pay handsomely."

The campfire crackled on the outskirts of Chelmsford. Matthew Hopkins had parked his carriage and horses just outside of town, on the edge of the forest. It was here that he and John Stearne had set up a small camp.

Sitting on logs around the roaring fire, John Stearne sloppily ate the chicken he'd been roasting over it. "So," he said with his mouth full, "he wants us to put on a show?"

"Hmm," Hopkins shrugged, "I would say more of an educational presentation." He was flipping through his leather journal. "The local magistrate knows that witchfinders of our caliber cannot be everywhere at once, so he'd like us to teach the villagers how to repel those ghastly creatures so they never become a threat in the first place."

"Right! Brilliant!" John Stearne frowned a moment later. "Wait a minute...do we *know* how to prevent witches?"

"It's all in here," Hopkins gestured to the journal in his hands. "Don't worry, John. It's all under control."

Stearne stared at the journal. "How come you never

let me see that? You don't think it wouldn't be a good idea for us both to be up to speed?"

"It is in the best interest of neither party that all knowledge is shared," Hopkins snapped, closing the journal. His journal had been their guide since they had begun witch hunting. Hopkins claimed that it contained all of his father's notes on witchcraft, a trove of information that made them the best at what they did. But Hopkins never let Stearne touch it.

"That makes no sense to me," Stearne said.

"If both sides know everything the other side does, then there is no *need* for two sides then, is there?"

Stearne took a moment to think about it. It made odd sense. If no one knows everything, then they have more motivation to stick together...and not betray each other.

"It's not that I don't trust you, my friend," Hopkins said sweetly. "It's that...I don't want to have to kill you. It would break my heart."

"Sure it would." Stearne rolled his eyes. "I'm retiring." He stood up and headed to his tent on the other side of the carriage. "Let's put on a good show."

"We sure will." Hopkins chuckled. "We sure, sure will." He looked down into his journal, which he coveted so deeply and violently protected from the eyes of others.

For the journal not only contained the techniques to finding and preventing witches, but also a secret that could, if exposed, change the world forever.

-9-

GOPHERS AND RABBITS

JULY 1645

The next morning, a drizzle engulfed the town of Chelmsford. At the town magistrate's office, John Gaule was having a chat with the clerk. At the moment, he was naming off every victim of yesterday's execution. Gaule was looking for one he recognized, but it never came.

"Is twenty-three the most you've ever hanged at once?" Gaule asked.

"We can be a little theatrical. Like to make a ceremony of it. Leave them up for a few days as a warning to others."

"I see. And instead of humanely using the gallows to snap their necks and cause instant release, you chose to string them up like hides in a butcher's shop, strangling them till death?"

"That is correct," the clerk said smugly.

Gaule sighed and cursed in Latin. "Fine," he said. "At least point me in the direction of one of their homes so I can see what this Mr. Hopkins may have found there."

"Why don't you ask Hopkins yourself?"

"Excuse me?"

"He's still in town, you know. About to give a presentation on keeping witches at bay."

Gaule was taken aback. He thought Hopkins would be far out in front of them by now. Perhaps, he thought, it was a blessing. "Where? And when?" Gaule demanded.

"I, uh, I think right now." The clerk nodded to the window. "Right up the street."

Gaule ran outside and looked up the road, where there was indeed a crowd gathering. He found Rebecca beneath the tree in the town center. She was sitting in the grass, looking up at the 23 corpses still dangling from its branches. Their bodies twisted in the breeze, picked at by birds and insects. The dead formed a forest of corpses beneath the tree.

"They look so peaceful in death," Rebecca said, staring upwards. "Do you think they are?"

"It depends," Gaule replied.

"On what?"

"Well," he shrugged, "on where they believe they deserve to be."

A rat suddenly appeared on Rebecca's shoulder, squeaking and tugging at her hair.

"Um, Rebecca..." Gaule stared at the rat.

"Don't worry, he's friendly," she said.

"Has it been travelling with us the whole time?"

"He certainly didn't fly here." She smiled.

"Right." Gaule leaned in and squinted at the rodent. "I've always understood that rats were much more intelligent than we give them credit for."

"Yes, but please don't pet him. I can't assure you he won't bite. He doesn't know you yet."

"Noted." Gaule stood up. "I think I will have no trouble avoiding petting him...Now, let's go."

"Where are we going?" Rebecca got up and brushed the grass off her clothes.

Before he replied, he started up the road as quickly

as he could. Rebecca stumbled behind him, eventually catching up. "Are you going to tell me where we're going?"

"It appears," Gaule said, "that Mr. Hopkins is not the ghost I was beginning to imagine he was."

They stopped at the edge of a large crowd that had gathered around a stage usually reserved for displaying vegetables on offer from local farmers. A sign was hung over the stage, adorned with the word "Demonology" written in faded ink.

On stage, Matthew Hopkins was already speaking. Gaule caught him mid-sentence:

"...indeed there are a number of ways to make my services redundant." Hopkins walked back and forth on stage as curious villagers looked on. "The best way to stop witches, is to prevent witches. Luckily, there are a number of techniques that one can use to help keep the demons away."

Hopkins turned to Stearne and snapped toward his shoe. "Please let me borrow your boot, Mr. Stearne."

"Um," Stearne wasn't quite expecting that. "Alright..." He took off his boot and tossed it to Hopkins.

"The shoe," Hopkins said to the crowd, "is with us all day. In the winters, all night. We have a bond with them. Our essence imbued in the leather. Put this shoe in your chimney. It will attract the witch there, where she will be stuck and die slowly."

There were nods of approval in the crowd. One man raised his hand and asked, "Sir, what if the witch is more cunning?"

"Ah, then we resort to stronger means," Hopkins said. "In this case, we may want to use a witch bottle. I have taken the liberty of having Mr. Stearne prepare one earlier." He nodded to John Stearne, who handed him a ceramic vase. Hopkins shook it. A liquid sloshed inside. "This bottle represents the bladder of the witch. If you feel you are being stalked by one of those vile creatures, targeted, perhaps, then fill it with your own urine. There exists a link between the fluids of the witch and her prey. By filling the bottle with your urine, you are creating a link with her bladder. Simply fill the bottle with nails..." Hopkins did so, letting some bent, rusty nails fall into the urine. "And now you have the witch in pain so excruciating that they will leave you to be."

More hands went up. More questions. Hopkins answered every one with the confidence of a snake oil salesman. He was a true showman.

And showmen, as Gaule knew, were also always liars. And he was determined to prove it.

When the show had ended, Hopkins answered a few more questions from individual villagers and collected tips in his hat. When the crowd had dispersed, he packed up his winnings and headed for a local tavern.

"Stay here," Gaule told Rebecca. "I'm going to go have a chat with our friend."

"And what am *I* supposed to do?" she whined.

"I don't know. Keep yourself occupied."

"Maybe I'll just whore myself out for the afternoon." There was clear sarcasm in her voice.

"Whatever." Gaule shrugged.

"Wait, what? You're supposed to tell me *not* to do that!" Rebecca scowled.

"Child, we were a historically matriarchal society up until recently. The whole idea of witches was invented by insecure men not wanting women more intelligent than them upsetting the newfound patriarchy's foundations. So as far as I'm concerned, Rebecca, if you can exert control over someone else using what little resources society hasn't stripped of you, then go for it."

"Um...alright."

"Stay here." Gaule jogged across the road and disappeared into the pub, leaving Rebecca alone in the center of town, staring up at the hanging corpses swinging beneath the enormous tree.

Moonlight Inn housed Chelmsford's premier tavern. It was where what could best be called the nobility of Chelmsford drank. Judges, magistrates, bankers. And on this day, they also hosted the esteemed Witchfinder General, who sat at the bar alone, downing a flagon of beer.

"Bit early for the drink, is it not?" John Gaule took a seat at the bar next to Matthew Hopkins.

"Nothing in the Bible against it," Hopkins replied grouchily, clearly having no interest in entertaining company.

"Is there not?" Gaule ordered a pint. "It is my

understanding that wine mocks those who use it, with the drink bringing nothing but woe and sorrow."

"'And in the end, it bites like a snake and poisons like a viper.'" Matthew Hopkins rolled his eyes. "I take the warnings as recommendations, not rules. And besides, I revel in woe and sorrow." Thunder rumbled outside. The rain picked up. A draft from outside swung the oil lamps. "You're a man of God, clearly."

"I am." Gaule took a sip of beer. "Are you?"

"Of course I am," Hopkins growled, noting the clergyman downing the alcohol with the pace of a common sinner.

"Could have fooled me."

"Did you not see the tree?" Hopkins nodded to the door, where outside the large tree in the center of town awaited. "Twenty-three traitors to God sent to Hell. All thanks to me."

"Well, congratulations. I hope your soul is clean."

Hopkins stared the vicar down. "Who are you?"

"John Gaule. Perhaps you've heard of me."

"I have." Hopkins smiled. "You're the one who's been spreading rumors about my work."

"Hmm." Gaule raised his eyebrows. "From what I've seen of your little travelling show, the 'rumors' painted you in a much better light than you could ever possibly deserve."

Hopkins laughed. He looked at the innkeeper and ordered two more drinks. One for himself and one for Gaule. "Do you want to hear a story from my childhood?"

"I imagine that's not a depressing tale at all considering we are sitting in the shadows of twenty-three corpses you are somehow *proud* of putting there."

"I can assure you that I had a very happy childhood, Mr. Gaule."

"That's...actually surprising." Gaule shrugged and took another sip.

"One winter, though, we had a bit of a gopher problem," Hopkins reflected. "They were nibbling at our crops, you see. Completely destroying everything we had worked so hard at for their own selfish gain."

"Survival," Gaule nodded in amusement. "How dare they."

"The beasts survived many years without stealing our crops, they can go back to it. Anyway," continued Hopkins, "my father had ordered my brother John and I to eliminate the gophers. Smoke them out, you see. Only then would our garden proliferate and prosperity return. But there was a problem."

"A witch problem?"

"Not exactly. It appeared that a family of rabbits had taken to using the tunnels that the gophers had dug. One of my younger brothers had taken a liking to the rabbits, but unfortunately I could not poison the gophers without also killing the rabbits."

"I see," Gaule nodded. "You felt the marks on your soul were not outweighed by the potential rewards."

"Correct." Hopkins downed half his flagon of beer in a few mighty gulps before proudly slamming it down on the counter. "I killed everything in the tunnels, Gaule. Because if a few innocents were killed in the name of doing God's work, then so be it."

"God's never minded sacrifice, has He?" Gaule thought of all the times through the Bible that God had demanded a life, either as retribution or as a statement of trust in his eventual message. "You know, I really thought we were past such barbaric practices."

"You call it 'barbaric,'" Hopkins said, "I call it the work that softer men do not have the courage to do. I have no doubt that some innocent people have lost their lives under me, but just as our garden flourished after smoking the gopher tunnels, so too shall this world be cleansed." Hopkins pulled a large coin from his pocket and flipped it to the innkeeper.

"Funny," Gaule mused, watching the innkeeper stare at the coin in disbelief. Apparently he had purposely overpaid the man. "Cleansed of both its demons and its wallet, I see."

"I have a team to pay," Hopkins said. "Horses to feed. I cannot work effectively if I work for free. Let me ask you, what's a vicar's salary?"

"Enough."

"Which is all I ask for, as well." Hopkins stood, tipped his hat, and turned to leave.

"I think you're a fraud."

The Witchfinder General stopped dead in his tracks. He turned around to face the older man with fire in his eyes. "I beg your pardon?"

"You," Gaul spun on his barstool, "are a fraud."

Hopkins smiled. "And how is that?"

"Oh, please. You and I both know you're too smart to believe in this hogwash about witches and pacts with the Devil, Matthew. But you're a hell of a businessman. And a businessman without a conscience is a dangerous man."

"Hmm." Hopkins sighed. "Perhaps you are right, vicar. Perhaps I will come and confess for these sins of mine. You know, I do believe," he said threateningly, "that a trip is overdue to, where is it you preside? Great Staughton, is it?"

Gaule dropped his friendly façade and clenched his fists. "You will be brought to justice long before that, Hopkins. If you believe you'll hang any of my people for the sake of filling your own coffers, then this is not going to end the way you think."

"Or perhaps it won't end the way *you* think, Mr. Gaule." Hopkins cracked his knuckles. "You have the idea that I deal in fear. I actually take it as a compliment."

"Are you threatening a man of the church, Hopkins?" Gaule asked. "Because if you did, then perhaps I shall retract my statement about you being smart. You wouldn't be stupid enough to accuse a man of God, would you?"

"You see, the thing about fear, Mr. Gaule, is that it's like the flame of a candle. It spreads, and spreads, until nothing, not even the slivers of wax that thought they were safe beneath their own righteousness, shall be spared." Hopkins smiled. That dastardly, evil smile. "Have a fantastic afternoon, Mr. Gaule."

"Considering you're leaving, I imagine I shall."

Hopkins ignored the quip and tipped his hat once more before vanishing into the rain. Gaule gave him a few minutes, then sprinted out toward his horse in a panic, nearly tripping in the mud. When he reached the stables, he threw the door open to find Rebecca flipping through a pamphlet.

"I thought you were busy whoring?" Gaule asked as he mounted his horse.

"I wanted to!" Rebecca said. "But it sort of lost its appeal when you actually approved it."

"I was *kidding*."

"Oh…"

"Let's go," Gaule said. "We have to stay on their trail. Perhaps make a stop in Great Staughton and make some arrangements in case Mr. Hopkins decides to stop there, himself."

"Shame. I was just starting to enjoy myself." Rebecca hopped up onto her horse.

"Hopkins made a threat that wasn't exactly vague," Gaule said. "But I cannot imagine he's stupid enough to attack a member of the clergy."

Gaule explained the situation to Rebecca as they headed off into the rain, the horses following the trails left by Hopkins and his company. Gaule felt only half at ease. A witchfinder would never stoop to accusing a man of God of witchcraft. It would be enough to ruin one's reputation.

Unless, of course, as John Gaule would shortly discover, that witchfinder was as insane, and as ruthless, as Matthew Hopkins.

-10-

SEEDS OF EVIL

DECEMBER 1634

Matthew Hopkins, 14-years-old, bounced in the back of a horse-drawn carriage as it made its way down the wintry mountain road. Pine trees dusted with snow shimmered in the twinkling of the midnight stars. In the distance, nestled in a valley, the parish of Great Wenham sat peacefully, the flickering yellow of fireplaces and smoking chimneys making it a warm, utopian beacon on such a cold night.

The carriage slipped into the village as fast as it could, the horses galloping through the snow-lined streets. It finally stopped at a small house next to St. John's Church; the Hopkins family home.

Young Matthew Hopkins jumped out of the

carriage and sprinted for the front door. The driver shouted something about needing help with his bags, but Matthew ignored him and ran inside to find his five brothers already gathered in the living room, all apparently having been waiting for his arrival.

They sat in silence as the fire crackled.

"Where is he?" Matthew asked, his breathing heavy. Snowflakes melted in his hair. Tears were already running down his face.

"The bedroom," John Hopkins said glumly.

Matthew took off.

"Wait!" John grabbed Matthew's arm as he ran by. "Matthew, it's not pretty...Don't do this to yourself. Please. Let this one go."

"You sent for me so I can see him one last time," Matthew reminded him. "I'm fulfilling that."

"Yes, but," John turned to his brothers for support. None had anything to say. "We thought you'd be here earlier, when he was more healthy. Please, Matthew, I'm asking you to trust me. No good can come of you going into that room."

Matthew Hopkins did not listen. He ripped his arm away from his older brother and stormed into the bedroom. There, he saw a sight his eyes had hoped never to witness, one he could scarcely comprehend: lying in bed were what could best be described as the skeletal remains of his father. James Hopkins had been stricken with an illness for weeks. It had sapped him of energy and reduced him to an emaciated husk of a man, barely able to speak.

Matthew Hopkins could not imagine ever seeing his father in such a state. His skin was brittle and bruised. His face was white and wrinkled. His teeth were gone, leaving black gums. When Matthew held his father's hand, he could feel the bones beneath the thin layer of what little flesh remained.

"Matthew," his father whispered. It was clear by the weakness of his voice that James Hopkins was delicately balancing on the fence between the world of the living and that of the dead. It was only a matter of time before he fell completely into the void.

"I'm here, father," Matthew said.

"I cannot…say the same…for your brothers…"

"They do not deserve the honor of seeing you off, father," Matthew said with conviction.

"They do not. But you, child," James touched his

son's face. "You are a true warrior for God. God *needs* warriors. Especially in times such as these."

"Because of evil." Matthew nodded. "We can stop it. Together, father. We can stop it from spreading across our land."

"We must. It is too late...for me..." James lifted the blanket off his chest, where a mark lay burned into his flesh. It was a red, raised mark shaped like a twinkling star.

The mark of one afflicted by a witch.

"A witch..." Matthew Hopkins gasped. "A witch did this to you, father?!"

James Hopkins coughed and wheezed. His time in this world was coming to an end. "Listen, son. Evil is spreading. Sin...it's like...a seed...a seed of evil. You must stop it. At *any* cost."

"Any cost, father," Matthew repeated.

"There is...a secret."

"A secret?"

James Hopkins gasped for breath. The mark on his chest burned and throbbed.

Matthew scrambled about, flustered, looking for

medicine or a pillow or a glass of water...anything to relieve his father's suffering.

"Forget it, child! Come here." James called his son over. "Fear is a powerful tool. Use it. Use it to stamp out the seeds of evil."

"I...I understand," Matthew said.

"No...you don't." James gestured to a journal on the nearby table. "That book. Bring it to me."

Matthew did as he was told. It was the same worn, leather journal he'd use in his later career. The same one he'd carry everywhere and let no one else see.

"There is a secret...inside this book," James said. "It is for your eyes only. Do you understand?"

Matthew hesitated. The gravity of what was about to happen had not yet dawned on him. James handed him the journal. It felt heavy. He took it gently. "Is this...*Daemonologie*?" he asked.

"No, no, it's...something else. Open it."

Matthew sat next to his father and opened the notebook. What he saw confused him at first and he demanded an explanation. And with his dying breaths, James Hopkins provided one.

-11-
FOURTEEN WIDOWS

AUGUST 1645

The waters of the North Sea boiled beneath a stormy sky. Rogue waves the size of monsters slammed against the hull of Nicholas Swift's schooner, *Remembrance*. Water spilled over the main deck as her small crew of six men braced for every impact, grabbing onto anything they could. They'd been fishing off the coast of Harwich when the storm hit. It had been like nothing the men had ever seen; swells taller than any they had ever experienced and rain like thick white sheets, as if conjured by God.

Or something else…

"Bring in the sails!" Swift shouted over the storm.

One of Swift's men sloshed through the water on

deck, slipping on some rope and smacking his face on a rail. When he got up, his nose was bleeding. He stumbled through the rain before collapsing at the bottom of the main mast.

"Christ, I'll do it myself!" Swift leapt down from his perch behind the ship's wheel and made his way to the mast. It wasn't an easy trip. On more than one occasion, a wave threatened to capsize the ship and he had to reach for some kind of handhold; a rope, a railing, anything.

"Captain!" one of his men yelled over the torrential downpour. "A ghost!"

A ghost?

Swift struggled to stand, gripping the wet railing as he looked out into the white sea. He scanned what little he could of the horizon, most of it obscured by the storm. Then, he saw it. Like a beast from the depths, the thing was gigantic, at least as large as their ship. It moved, a gray blob behind the wall of rain that grew bigger and bigger...

"It's coming for us!" one of the men shouted.

He was right. The creature appeared to be heading straight for their ship. It was coming at them fast.

Swift ran for the ship's wheel, though he knew in the back of his mind it would be too late. He slipped and slid his way up the steps and got behind the wheel, then looked up at the shape that had been approaching them through the storm.

It was another ship.

"Brace for impact!"

The other schooner *slammed* into *Remembrance* with the force of an angry leviathan. Wood exploded and the mast creaked and fell, snapping the second ship in two.

It was on that day that 14 men met their end in the abyss. As the schooners sank, they dragged their crews with them into the deep, cold, black waters.

Never to be seen again.

The congregation sang and prayed. The church of All Saints, located in Brandeston, was holding a vigil for those lost in the terrible accident off the coast of Harwich two weeks earlier. Those in attendance included the 14 widows of the men whose souls were lost. Many were accompanied by bawling children. Some were too young to understand that their fathers were not coming back.

The vicar, John Lowes, lit 14 candles at the front of the church. He was 80 years old and had proved to be a divisive member of the community. A widower, John Lowes had preferred traditional Anglicanism more than anything else, which had angered many of the parish's residents. Many of them felt that he was not extreme enough.

Anglicanism was known colloquially as "the middle way." It borrowed elements from Catholicism and Puritanism. For people who cared not for either extreme, it offered a good balance. However, during times of war, there was no middle ground. Those who were not exclusively with one were the enemy of the other. That isn't something that has changed much today, unfortunately, and it's what made John Lowes a controversial figure in his community. His refusal to bow to the pressure of Puritanism that fueled half the civil war was the reason he was so disliked among the villagers of Brandeston.

When confronted about these inadequacies, John Lowes was defensive. He frequently berated the younger members of his church and had a strict policy against allowing children into Sunday mass. John Lowes *hated* children. His curmudgeon attitude and unlikable nature had made him a frequent target of townsfolk, almost all of whom wanted him replaced. The problem, however, was that replacing a vicar was a difficult task.

There had to be…cause for removal.

After the evening had died down and the mourners left, Lowes extinguished the candles, one by one. When he was finished, he heard a clapping behind him. He turned to see a single man sitting amongst the church pews. It was a bearded man with a top hat and cape. He smiled and clapped.

"Excellent eulogy," Matthew Hopkins said. "I almost imagined, for a moment, that your concern for the souls of the young men lost at sea was, well how do I put this, genuine."

"And how do you know it wasn't?" Lowes asked, his voice cracking under the weight of his advanced age.

"I've spoken to villagers," Hopkins said. "I've come to understand that you were not at all fond of the sailors whom most tragically drowned off Harwich."

"Hmph." John Lowes adjusted the cross on his neck and began extinguishing the oil lamps around the church. "My personal feelings are irrelevant. I gave them what they needed to ensure they passed on peacefully to the next world. Where that next world is...well, I guess that depends on what those morons did in life."

"Morons, you say?" Hopkins stood up and clasped his hands behind his back. "Tell me, did you have problems with these men, Mr. Lowes?"

"Of *course* I did," Lowes snapped. "They were mean-spirited, bigoted men who caused so much raucous after a pint at the local tavern that I'd have trouble even sleeping!"

"They were young."

"And stupid. And an interruption. Good riddance."

Hopkins glared. "You sound like a man who wanted them gone."

"I want no one gone. But if God wills it, and it just

so happens to benefit me, then I won't complain." Lowes left one oil lamp lit, as was his tradition, in case he had to return to the church in the middle of the night.

It was dark inside.

Dark enough for the eyes of Matthew Hopkins to glow in the flickering light of the single lamp. Eyes that stared at the old vicar like a bull at the red cape of a matador. "John Lowes," Hopkins barked, "you have been formally accused of conspiring with the Devil to cause the untimely deaths of those you deemed less worthy."

Lowes's eyes went wide. "Lies! I would *never* stoop to such a thing!"

"Fourteen experienced seamen perished over a mistake an amateur would not have made!" Hopkins approached the old vicar, producing a set of iron handcuffs.

"They were drunken fools!" Lowes eyed the cuffs with fear. "Their fate was brought upon themselves by their own decisions!"

"I don't believe you," Hopkins growled.

Lowes, his body long past the era of its youthful

flexibility, fell to the ground and tried to crawl away. But it was no use. Hopkins grabbed the old man by the shoulders and flipped him onto his back before forcing the handcuffs over his bony, wrinkled fingers. Lowes stopped struggling and wailed in agony as Hopkins picked him up, slinging him over his shoulder like a sack of spice.

Outside, John Stearne was waiting by the carriage. He was stunned to see Matthew Hopkins carrying back not a random churchgoer, as he had expected, but a man dressed in holy robes.

"Matthew!" Stearne whispered with panic as Hopkins opened the back of the carriage and slung the fainted vicar inside. "What madness is this? A priest?!"

"No one is above the law of God." Hopkins slammed the carriage door shut and locked it tight. "Not a priest. Not even a witch hunter." He gave John Stearne a threatening look. "Now, are you going to relieve yourself of your concerns, Mr. Stearne, and join me as I take this prisoner to Bury Saint Edmunds, or are you going to let your behavior instigate a search of your body for Devil's Marks?"

John Stearne gulped. "No, sir. I'm with you every step of the way."

"Good." Hopkins slipped on his gloves and climbed up behind the horses. "Because as I am a patient man, I am also a man who is not afraid to act in his own best interests, should the need arise. Do you understand, Mr. Stearne?"

"I do." Stearne sighed and climbed up next to Matthew Hopkins. "I just hope we are careful not to stray too far from God's will."

"My friend," Hopkins smiled and cracked the horse whip, "we *are* God's will."

-12-
MAKING MONSTERS

AUGUST 1645

TWO WEEKS AFTER THE ARREST OF JOHN LOWES

Rebecca West hummed as her and Gaule's horses galloped down a long stretch of road, miles of endless fields surrounding them in all directions. In the distance, they could see a mountain range. Below that, a plume of smoke rising into the air. Gaule hoped that was smoke from the chimneys of their destination: Bury St Edmunds, the last place they had heard Hopkins was heading.

"How much *longer?*" Rebecca asked with an exaggerated sigh.

"Another hour, I imagine," Gaule replied. "Maybe two. Are you bored?"

"You have no idea," Rebecca said. "Maybe to a

degree which could be considered child abuse given the right mixture of crocodile tears in a courtroom."

"A child." Gaule chuckled. "You call yourself one. I don't buy it."

"And why is that?" Just as Rebecca asked, her pet rat emerged from her pack and took its familiar spot on her shoulder. "Is it because you consider rodents to be pets for children?"

"Or food for dogs."

The rat twitched, as if it had somehow understood him. Rebecca calmed it down, stroking its fur. "Now, now, he was just joking."

"The intelligence of those animals has always surprised me," Gaule said, glancing at the rat. "I've papers indicating that they could possibly outmatch the cerebral abilities of a housecat."

Rebecca smirked. "'Cerebral abilities.' You are sure you are a man of faith and not one of science?"

Gaule shrugged. "I've never believed in the two being mutually exclusive. It is my belief that they have always complemented one another in various ways. Two ideas telling the same story in different languages. Trust me, Ms. West. I am a man of faith. I pray to God, and he sometimes answers. I use faith to steer men and women toward, I don't know, a *good* path. That is why I believe in my faith."

"I still do not understand," Rebecca said. "Are you a man of spirit or a man of science?"

"Few things in this world cannot be explained scientifically. That is a reality that I have come to accept. But I am not ruling out God just because I can see the blocks with which he constructed our world. Science, Rebecca, provides the tools and ingredients that God uses. He is the answer to why. Science, I believe, is the answer to how."

Rebecca suddenly stopped her horse. Gaule, caught off-guard, stopped his a few meters up the road and turned around to face her. She was staring at the vicar with firm intent.

"Rebecca, what's wrong?"

"What are you doing here?" she asked without a hint of playfulness in her voice.

"Excuse me?"

"*You*. John Gaule. Why are you so determined to stop Matthew Hopkins? What do you get out of this?

Shouldn't you be…be…I don't know…seeing to your church in Great Staughton?"

Thunder bellowed as lightning lit the sky on fire. The first raindrops of the coming storm began to fall. Gaule approached Rebecca and then got off his horse. He looked shaken. "Perhaps, we should make camp and wait for the rain to pass."

Twenty minutes later, Gaule had set up a large tent made of a fabric he'd purchased from a travelling salesman who'd promised it was waterproof. Gaule had the idea to use it to cover some of the more valuable outdoor statues in his church's garden. However, it also turned out to make a great shelter from the elements. While far from completely waterproof, it did provide enough resistance to allow their campfire to roar.

Gaule ate while Rebecca stared at him from the other side of the fire, their shadows flickering off the walls of the tent as the storm raged just outside.

"You never answered my questions," Rebecca reminded him. "A habit of yours, I'm quickly learning. Mr. Gaule, what made you wake up one day and decide to chase this cause? Especially as a man whose faith seems to be in conflict with that of everyone else?"

"First off," Gaule gulped his food, "my faith is *not* in conflict. I don't know how many times I need to tell people that I am still a stringent believer."

"Then why hunt the witch hunters?"

"Because I also believe in good. The good of my faith. The good of my church. And what Hopkins is doing, by allowing blind conviction to take control of his common sense, will *destroy* our faith."

"I don't understand." Rebecca shook her head. "This hunting of witches, of those who deal with the Devil, how will that destroy your faith? Will it not strengthen it?"

Gaule finished his food and sighed. "We live in a world of opposing sides, Rebecca. That's a good thing. It means that people are beginning to think for themselves. The problem is that, when you have sides of a conflict, whether it be something as simple as incense or no incense in a church, both sides will ultimately convince themselves that they are right, and that the opposing side is wrong. End of story. People too often see the world in black and white. But you and I, we know different. We know the world doesn't work that way. The real world is filled with shades of gray. And that makes people uncomfortable. Having to accept the possibility that their own ideas might not ultimately be the right ones."

"You're assuming human beings don't compromise," Rebecca said.

"Yeah, I'm feeling fairly safe in that assumption. Not only do they not compromise, but they don't empathize. Instead they often choose to demonize." Gaule smirked and shook his head. "We live in a world where if someone has a different idea or perspective from our own, we make no attempt to listen or initiate dialogue. No, we create our assumption of this person's entire character over a difference of perspective, and we treat them as a monster."

Rebecca dipped her head. She, too, had been guilty of immediately dismissing someone over having an opinion different than her own.

"And let me tell you something, Rebecca. The fastest way to create a real monster, is to make someone into one in your head. When you shout at, scream at, or persecute people for having a perspective you do not understand, they get scared. They lash out."

He looked at the girl across the fire. "Hopkins thinks he will strengthen the church. But he will not. No one is going to let themselves be demonized, then wake up going, 'Yes, the people threatening me, *that's* the side I want to be on!' Even if you are one hundred percent right and they are one hundred percent wrong, no good can ever come from antagonizing those who disagree. You do nothing but throw logs on the flames of your own burning cause. Hate will always ensure only one thing: more hate."

"I'm beginning to understand." Rebecca crossed her arms. "You're afraid that Hopkins will turn people away from the word of God."

Gaule nodded. "From the corpses of a thousand monsters that Hopkins has slayed in his head, there will eventually rise real ones. Angry, scared monsters. I will not let my faith be destroyed. Not by Hopkins. Not by anyone. That is my duty."

"Why is he doing this?" Rebecca asked. "Hopkins.

Does he truly believe himself to be some kind of crusader?"

Gaule's memory flashed back to several weeks ago. When he was sitting next to Hopkins at a tavern in Chelmsford. "There is pain in his eyes," Gaule said. "There are two types of drinkers in this world."

"You mean those who consume alcohol?" Rebecca said with a condescending tone. "Oh, what *ever* does that do? Little old innocent me has no earthly idea!"

"Uh huh." Gaule waved her off. "Anyway, Rebecca, the two types of drinkers in this world are those who drink for fun..."

Rebecca smiled.

"...and those who drink to forget. I, I have been both in my life. I can recognize the eyes of both, as I've spent many nights staring into my own reflection, trying to come to terms with what my life had become. Matthew Hopkins was drinking that day in Chelmsford to forget."

"Do you think he feels guilt for the things he has done? Or perhaps does he not even truly believe? Maybe this hunt has been an elaborate money-making scheme and the marks on his soul are finally beginning to burn his insides. Maybe he's human, after all."

"Maybe," Gaule sighed. "I'd love to know myself. There's a notebook he carries around. A leather one. Worn."

"I've seen it," Rebecca confirmed. "He was reading from it when doing that stupid show with the shoe and the piss bottle."

"Yes. I have a feeling that we will find answers in that notebook. Answers to everything. Maybe even something to incriminate the man so he cannot harm again. I'm sure parliament will be on my side in a case such as this."

"Is that what you're hoping for?" asked Rebecca. "Or are you really hoping that you will find something in that book to exonerate his soul from its crimes? Maybe, just maybe," she made a pinching motion with her fingers, "you're just trying too hard to find the good in everyone."

"Something that I'm finding more difficult with each passing day, unfortunately."

"I have something to tell you, Mr. Gaule. I do not

want you to be alarmed." She pulled herself closer to the fire, closer to Gaule. They watched each other through an undulating curtain of flames. "I was fond of my mother. She was a good woman. She did not deserve an early death, let alone such a grisly one at the hands of a man who spent what he earned for her life on breakfast."

Gaule knew where this was going. He knew this was a bridge he'd have to cross eventually. But he was hoping he had more time.

"I do intend to bring harm to him," Rebecca West said. "He is a man who deserves not the air he breathes, yet alone the riches of fame to which he's grown accustomed. All I ask is that you do not try to stop me when that time comes."

"Hmph." Gaule knew that there was little use of attempting to reason with a broken heart. "Perhaps I won't have to. Perhaps, if that time comes, God will stop you."

"God has no control over me," Rebecca said. "I refuse to believe anyone has control over me. No parent. No man. No magistrate."

Gaule nodded. "That explains many things about you."

"What things? Hmm?"

"Your fire, for one."

"I just hate the idea of tradition determining my place in life. I don't want to get married at sixteen and spend my days kneading dough while my husband works in a field."

"The world is changing, Rebecca. For the better, I assure you." Gaule said. "But I understand that it is far from easy to look at things through a certain lens, or attempt to experience things through a different body. It is unfortunately quite difficult for people to see people different than them as people at all. We just see others as...objects...pawns in this great game of life which we are all playing."

"Everyone expects certain things of me," Rebecca said, seemingly ignoring Gaule's last insufferable diatribe. "I have to be *proper* and hope a boy *chooses me* as if I'm some sort of prize to be won in a tournament. I'm expected to want to have children and raise a family. Anything else, like wanting to see the world, or, or to study nature or mathematics and suddenly—"

"You're a witch."

"Yes." Rebecca sounded exasperated, on the verge of tears. "I don't want other people to look down on me when I don't do what *they* want me to do. It drives me mad. It makes me feel lost. I do not want to be controlled. Not by you. Not by a county. Not by *anyone*. God gave me my life, and I trust he also gave me the sense, and the freedom, to use it how I so choose. I've done a few bad things. Sure. What of it? Condemn me. I don't care."

"Child," Gaule said, "we have *all* done bad things. What's important is not so much what we have done, but *why* we have done it. One day, you will understand. I promise. You are a remarkable human being, Rebecca West. And remarkable not because you stick to convention, but because you don't. Do not let the world tell you who you are. Let your actions show them."

Rebecca sniffled. "Thank you."

"For what?"

"For calling me remarkable."

Gaule walked over and hugged the young woman. She hugged back even harder. He got the distinct impression that it was the first time anyone had listened to anything she had to say in quite some time.

Outside, the horses stirred. It appeared that the storm had passed. "It's time," Gaule said. "Let's head to the village."

As the two packed up the tent and rode off toward Bury St Edmunds, neither had any idea that they were about to witness perhaps the most heinous and iconic act of the career of Matthew Hopkins.

-13-
SINKING GUILT

AUGUST 1645

John Gaule and Rebecca West rode into town an hour after packing their tent, only to find that a large crowd had already gathered at the base of a castle. There seemed to have been a commotion at the lake right next to the castle, and villagers looked on curiously at something along its muddy banks.

Gaule and Rebecca West tied down their horses and rushed to see what was going on, rudely pushing their way to the front of the crowd. When they arrived, they saw Matthew Hopkins standing at the end of a pier. And strung up on rope like a fish was an old man. He didn't writhe or cringe. In fact, he didn't move at all; he looked completely defeated.

"This so-called *priest*, a supposed defender of our faith," started Matthew Hopkins to the crowd. "This man has been accused of making a pact with the Devil to take the lives of fourteen innocent men off the coast of Harwich. Vicar John Lowes did not *like* these men because of their drinking habits. Their desire to have a little fun *offended* him." He looked to the crowd for approval. Many of them nodded. "And as such, he is accused of having had them eliminated."

"A witch!" came cries from the crowd. "To the gallows!"

"Now, now." Hopkins patted the air, a gesture to his crowd to calm down. "We are a civilized society with civilized rules. You see, John Lowes here has been a faithful servant of his church for many decades. It is my belief, as should be *all* of ours, that he deserves the benefit of the doubt. Four days of sleep deprivation did not yield a confession. So, I have decided to turn to more drastic measures."

The night before, Matthew Hopkins was in a panic. He had just accused a member of the clergy of witchcraft, so he was already playing an incredibly dangerous game. But now, the old man, after four continuous days without sleep, was *still* not confessing. The magistrate was running out of patience, and Hopkins knew that if he had falsely accused a priest of such a terrible crime, he'd never be taken seriously again.

You must have the strength to do what is necessary.

Matthew heard the words of his father ringing in his head.

It is easy to give your life to a cause. It is much more difficult to give your soul.

Matthew knew that his soul had long since gone. He also knew that unless he extracted a confession from the vicar as quickly as possible, it would derail his mission.

So, ever the clever man, he came up with a solution.

And that's what led to the vicar John Lowes being hung up like meat over the lake. The rope was connected to a pulley on the pier, which was itself connected to a winch.

"John Lowes," Hopkins said, "has renounced his baptism as a condition of his pact with the Devil." He was reading from his leather journal, a fact that had not gone unnoted by both Rebecca West and John Gaule. "Therefore," continued Hopkins, "water, being a substance so pure that it rejects evil beings, will tell us whether John Lowes is truly in league with dark forces. If the man sinks, he will be proclaimed innocent. But if he floats, then there will be only one explanation as to why."

Gaule shook his head. *I can think of a million scientific explanations off the top of my head!*

Rebecca looked over at Gaule. "I don't understand. People float all the time. Witch or no witch."

"People will see," Gaule sighed, "what they *want* to see. We will trick our minds into believing what we want to believe."

Hopkins yanked on the winch. Lowes dropped a few feet toward the water before Hopkins pulled it taut again. Then, he kicked the winch and the man *plummeted* into the lake with a splash. He writhed and screamed and spat out water.

All while, apparently, floating on its surface.

The crowd cried out in triumph. "I knew he was a witch!" "Let him burn!" "Convict!"

One of the men from the crowd walked out onto the

pier. He appeared to be one of the town's magistrates, there to attend the dunking. "Mr. Hopkins," the magistrate said, "need I remind you that we will need a *confession* to convict."

"Despite this obvious *proof!*" Hopkins nodded to the struggling Lowes. The effect was quite mesmerizing. The vicar was writhing on top of the water as if they were separated by a sheet of clear glass, his robes barely touching the surface.

"Proof is not a confession, Mr. Hopkins."

"Alright," Hopkins snarled. "I have the impression that Mr. Lowes is about to give us that very confession."

In the water, unnoticed by many due to his squirming and twitching, Lowes sank.

Just a little.

Just enough.

"Do we have that confession, Mr. Lowes?!" Hopkins asked from the pier.

There was no confession. Only muffled gurgling as he fought to keep water out of his mouth. A moment later, his body was lowered even more, and more, until he felt a moment of terror so extreme that he would have blurted out anything to escape from drowning: "I confess!"

"What's that?" Hopkins cupped his hand over his ear.

"I confess!" shouted Lowes. "I confess!"

Hopkins gave a knowing glance to the magistrate. "I believe that should suffice."

"Right." The magistrate looked back toward his three fellow men of the court. They all nodded. "Mr. Lowes," the magistrate said, "you are hereby found guilty of the crime of communing with the Devil and will be sentenced to death."

At the gallows stood 18 souls. John Godbolt, a portly man who ran the local court and had ordered the witch trials, paced back and forth along a stage, reading out the names of those sentenced to death by hanging. He was nearing the end of the list. "Mary Clowes. Mary Fuller. Anne Alderman. Anne Leech. And finally, John Lowes."

The 80-year-old man, still dripping wet from his dunking, stood at the end of the line of the condemned, which consisted mostly of crying middle-aged women, begging to be spared, their pleas falling on deaf ears who had already decided, in their own minds, that their lives would be better without these people around.

"We will begin with you, Mr. Lowes. Out of respect for your years of service to the church, we will spare you the pain of watching your partners in evil be punished." Godbolt nodded to an executioner, who started toward the old priest.

"Wait!" a voice rang up from the crowd. Godbolt looked down to see a man in his late 30s rushing toward the stage, followed by a young woman who couldn't have been half his age. "Wait! Just one moment!"

Gaule climbed to the stage and addressed the confused crowd of onlookers. "You're making a terrible mistake. This is a man of God!" He gestured to Lowes. "I know this because I am one myself. I am John Gaule, vicar of Great Staughton."

"And I'm Rebecca West!" Rebecca climbed onto the stage and stood next to him. "I...um...I...I also do things. Sometimes."

Boos erupted from the audience.

"Good people, listen!" Gaule stepped forward. "This has gone too far! This man has appeared out of nowhere and suddenly you're executing priests? On his word?"

"John Lowes despised my husband," a woman from the crowd yelled up. "He had him killed. I cannot let this pass."

"So, it's vengeance you want?" Gaule asked. "Vengeance is a blinding poison. Please. I am asking you to use *reason*. Do not harm these innocent people. Their lives should not be forfeit over coincidence."

It was no use. The crowd shouted curses toward the stage. They wanted blood and they wanted it now.

"Son," Lowes said. Gaule turned. He was surprised that the old man was able to speak. "You will only throw suspicion onto yourself. Please. Let it go."

"I *cannot* let it go," Gaule boiled. "I *cannot*."

"You *must*. You can do no good here," Lowes said. "Live to fight another day."

Before he could answer, Gaule was picked up by the gigantic executioner and thrown into the crowd, who dispersed while his body was in the air and let him land in the muck, facedown in mud. He sat up and spat out dirt.

The executioner moved toward Rebecca.

"Uh, no need," she said, stepping off the stage of her own free will. "I'll go ahead and volunteer..."

From the ground, Gaule watched as Lowes was kicked off the stage. He was lucky. His life ended with but a single *snap*. A few twitches later, he was gone.

"Dammit." Gaule grabbed the cross around his neck and closed his eyes tight. *They'd gone too far.* When he looked up, he met the gaze of Matthew Hopkins, who'd been standing at the back of the crowd. He was flipping some coins up and down in his palm and smiling.

In that instant, something changed in Gaule. Perhaps he had reached his limit. But in that moment, he was no longer a man, but a beast. He leapt to his feet and chased after Hopkins, who suddenly found himself afraid of the animalistic bloodlust in his enemy's eyes.

Gaule, who was never much of a fighter, threw

himself at Matthew Hopkins, knocking him into the mud. There, the two fought. Punches were thrown...and some even landed. Gaule eventually got the better of Hopkins, who appeared to be an even worse fighter than the clergyman, and pinned him on his back as villagers looked on.

"*Why are you doing this?!*" Gaule shouted.

Hopkins, half-choking, laughed. "Just to piss you off, John."

"*You're nothing but a murderer!*"

"I am doing what is necessary to defeat evil!"

Gaule, in an even rarer moment of white hot rage, picked a rock off the ground and raised it over Matthew's head. "So am I."

Wham!

Gaule felt his body go limp as the massive form of John Stearne smashed into him. After coming to his senses, Gaule suddenly found himself being arrested by one of the local magistrates.

"He attacked me," Hopkins said, picking himself off the ground and brushing off the dirt. "Attacked me without cause."

"I had cause," Gaule squabbled. "I have *dozens* of

causes. One of them just had his neck snapped so you could put a coin in your pocket!"

"I apologize, sir," the magistrate told Hopkins. "Would you like to press charges, sir?"

Gaule stared Hopkins down.

Hopkins smiled. "No, I would not. We wouldn't want to punish a man of God now, would we? Do me a favor, though, and hold him until I take my leave. I would like to pack my things without the threat of danger."

"Of course. Come on." The magistrate dragged John Gaule to the local prison, where he would sit for several hours. Gaule was not feeling gracious for Hopkins declining to press charges. No, it wasn't some gesture of good faith toward a clergyman; clearly, Hopkins had no qualms about killing men of God.

It was because, as Gaule knew, the sentence for assault was but a few weeks in prison.

But the sentence for witchcraft could be death.

Hopkins arrived at his carriage to find John Stearne waiting for him. "Let's go," Hopkins said. "There's always another witch to hang."

"Actually, uh, Mr. Hopkins," John said shakily. "I do not wish to go any farther with you."

"Excuse me?"

"The priest, sir. John Lowes. I...I think it was too far. And some of the villagers, I believe they feel the same, sir. It was a mistake. We may have angered God."

Hopkins stepped toward the significantly taller man, craning his neck to meet his eye line. His lack of height, however, did not make him any less menacing. "The only one you are angering is *me*."

"I'm sorry." Stearne shook his head. "I'm just...I'm sorry. I'm going back to my family."

"Your family, huh?" Hopkins smirked. "Well enjoy the money you made from your few months of exploiting God. Perhaps I shall pay Manningtree a visit soon."

Stearne glared. "I'm not afraid of you."

"Ah, the famous last words of many who have crossed my path," Hopkins replied. "Get out of here, John. Go back to your family. You are not *worthy* of being an arm of God."

"I think," Stearne said, "there's only one person standing here not worthy of anything. Goodbye, Matthew. Good luck with whatever it is you're looking for."

"I don't need your *luck*," Matthew said as Stearne walked away. "I have *God* on my side."

Rebecca smiled the widest smile she'd ever smiled in her entire life as the gate to John Gaule's prison cell was opened by the magistrate.

"Did you have fun?" she beamed.

Gaule rolled his eyes. "I did. Lots of time to think. And unfortunately lost time on capturing Hopkins. We'll have to ask around and figure out where he's heading next. One of the councilmen should be able to tell us. Albeit probably for most of the coin I have in my pocket…"

"Already taken care of."

"What?" Gaule looked surprised. "Really?"

Rebecca kissed one of her index fingers, then another, then touched them together seductively.

"Oh," Gaule said sheepishly. "I see…"

"Just consider it," Rebecca said, "my way of taking back control by using the few resources that society hasn't stripped of me."

-14-
IPSWICH WITCH

SEPTEMBER 1645

Henry Reade was in agony. Red sores covered his body, which glistened with sweat. The sores burned and itched. Some grew so massive on his throat that he could barely breathe. The young man of 22 was living in the embodiment of Hell's fire.

"How long has this been afflicting him?" a physician asked Henry's father, Edward Reade. The two were standing by the boy's bedside as he writhed in pain.

"It started last night, as soon as we got home from the tavern," answered Edward Reade. "Maybe something he drank?"

"I find that doubtful," said the physician. "If that were a factor, I fear we'd have many more than just this one case." The physician noticed a mark beneath the boy's neck, right at the spot where it met his chest. It was a raised, red mark the shape of a six-pointed star. "What in the Devil?"

Something clicked in Edward Reade's brain. "The Devil…"

"Did something…occur recently, Edward?"

"Yes…Henry, my boy…yesterday he…he broke off his engagement with Elizabeth Lakeland. Her grandmother was…very upset. She said…that not marrying her granddaughter had essentially put a pox on our family."

"Mary Lakeland?" the physician knew the name. The old woman was generally adored in the community and taught at the local church. Her reputation was spotless.

"Yes…" Edward Reade began to grow red with anger. "It was *her! She* did this to my son!"

"Let's calm down a second," the physician gently put his hands on Edward's shoulders. "That's a dangerous accusation to throw around, Edward. Especially without any evidence. Now, let's be gentlemen and we will go speak to Mary Lakeland ourselves, alright?"

Edward Reade took a deep breath and nodded. The two left Henry Reade in the care of his mother while they made the short trek across the village to the home of Mary Lakeland. Ipswich was a port town, and the sounds of bells and sailors in the harbor were ever-present. Seagulls cawed in the air and occasionally swooped down to steal the day's catch of fish. The homes and roads here were of better construction than most small cities thanks to the population's wealth.

Mary Lakeland was married to the local barber-surgeon, William Lakeland. Both were well-known figures in Ipswich. The physician knew that accusing Mary Lakeland of a crime was going to take tact and finesse. As they approached the home, which also served as the barber shop, the physician rehearsed lines in his head, hoping to make what they were going to suggest less insulting and more digestible. They were going to need a lot more evidence, that's for sure. Ipswich was a civilized town with civilized magistrates who required strict proof, and proof was always hard to find.

Or at least that's what he thought before he opened the door to the Lakeland barber shop that morning.

Mary Lakeland was on her knees, crying over the body of her husband. He lied on his back, staring at the ceiling with dead eyes.

The physician gulped, "Mrs. Lakeland...what happened!"

"I don't know!" Mary Lakeland cried. "I just found him like this! He's gone! He's gone!" On the back of her hand, both men noticed a large, bleeding cut. It was a clean cut, as if made by a blade.

Or a claw of the Devil.

Edward Reade and the physician gave each other looks of certainty. There was no such thing as coincidence.

Within an hour, Mary Lakeland was in jail, accused by Edward Reade of witchcraft; making a deal with the Devil to afflict the young Henry Reade with painful sores and tumors for the crime of ending his engagement to her granddaughter. The magistrates had also been convinced that her husband was going to turn her in for these crimes, so she killed him to keep him quiet.

Of course, she denied everything.

Meanwhile, Henry Reade continued to suffer.

Not knowing exactly what to do with Mary Lakeland, the magistrates discussed what their legal options were; could they execute without a confession? Without proof?

Then, like some twisted angel of blackness, Matthew Hopkins came stumbling into the magistrate's offices.

"Can we help you?" one of the magistrates asked, clearly annoyed by the intrusion.

"I understand you have apprehended a witch," Hopkins said. He was short of breath. His hair was messy. His beard dirty. He also reeked of alcohol and stumbled with a drunken gait.

"A *suspected* witch," the magistrate clarified. "Are you drunk, sir?"

"Drunk with experience. My name is Matthew Hopkins."

The magistrates recognized his name immediately.

It had been floated to nearly all the villages of East Anglia. He was a man whose services were always in demand and greatly respected.

"I apologize, Mr. Hopkins," the magistrate said. "Of course, we'd love to have your expertise."

After agreeing to a price, one of the magistrates led Matthew Hopkins to the prison cell where Mary Lakeland was being held. In the same cell was another woman. She was much younger, not much older than Rebecca.

"Ah, two, I see," Hopkins said.

"Who are you?" Mary Lakeland asked from the other side of the bars. "What do you want with us?"

"I am here to help, ma'am," Hopkins said. "Who is this charming young lady?"

The younger blonde sniffled. "Alice Denham."

"Alice," Hopkins smiled, "such a pretty name. Give me your hand, dear."

The girl hesitated.

Matthew calmly placed his hand through the bars. The girl finally took it. She was shaking.

"My job, young lady, is to get you off the proverbial hook, so to speak," Hopkins said. "It is my belief, of course, that you are innocent. And so, what I am going to do, is put you through some paces that will allow you both, undeniably, to prove your innocence." He opened the gate and stepped into their cell. Then, he opened his bag with a smile. "Are we ready to begin?"

Both women beamed with relief. This was a man, they thought, that truly cared for them. Both Alice Denham and Mary Lakeland were good people. Both were well-liked in their community and dedicated their lives to helping others.

It was a pity then, that in a few days, both would succumb to Hopkins' torture of sleep deprivation. Both would sign confessions for crimes they didn't commit. And both would experience the absolute worst punishment ever to befall an accused witch.

John Gaule and Rebecca West had arrived in Ipswich one day too late to interfere with Hopkins' interrogation and prevent the two accused from confessing. Word had come from the magistrates that the two had finally confessed and their fate would be decided by vote in the morning. Gaule and West were too late to stop the confession, but they weren't too late to get what they really came for.

After hearing from locals that Hopkins was renting a room at the Windward Inn, Rebecca used her powers of seduction to book the room right next to it. It was here that they waited for Hopkins to come home, then inevitably make his way down to the bar.

"Alright," Gaule said, opening the door. He looked over the balcony railing and down into the tavern. Hopkins was sitting alone at the bar. Gaule looked to Rebecca. "You know what to do?"

She nodded.

"You sure?"

"You think this is the first room I've ever broken into?"

"I was kind of hoping it would be." Gaule sighed. "No matter." He turned and looked back down at Hopkins again. This time, however, Hopkins was looking like he was getting ready to leave the bar and come back upstairs. Possibly for the rest of the night. Which would ruin their chances of getting what they needed. "Shit!" Gaule cursed. "Go, now! I'll keep Hopkins distracted!"

Gaule made his way downstairs while Rebecca picked the lock on Hopkins' room door and slipped inside.

"Mr. Hopkins!" Gaule beamed, rushing down the stairs and meeting Hopkins on his way up. "Another successful confession, I hear?"

Hopkins stared. He didn't smile. He didn't blink. His face looked tired. His eyes looked sunken. "What do you want, Gaule?"

"To apologize."

"For?"

"Everything. Socking you in the eye, for starters."

"It'll heal." Hopkins tried to move past him and up the stairs to his room.

"Wait, look, Matthew," Gaule sighed. "I wanted to come to a truce. Lately I have realized that you and I both want the same thing. The world to be free of sin. You have your way and I have mine. And tonight I'd like to ask you a favor."

"And what would that be?"

"Convince me," Gaule said.

"Of?"

"To help you."

Upstairs, Rebecca carried a lit candle around Matthew Hopkins' room at the inn. It was messier than she imagined. Hopkins had always carried himself with an air of nobility. He spoke and dressed like a gentleman, and Rebecca imagined he'd be impossibly charming if not for his penchant for mass murder.

Clothes lay strewn about. Feathers from pillows that had been slammed against the wall were scattered everywhere. And liquor bottles. Piles of empty liquor bottles could be found in every corner.

Someone had been quite angry.

Getting her mind back on her quest, she started shuffling around the desk. It was a mess of papers. Some had been torn apart. Perhaps broken contracts? She took a closer look. They weren't contracts. Many of the torn letters were letters from religious officials condemning the actions of Matthew Hopkins. There was even one that looked like it was formally stamped from parliament! Rebecca scanned the letter.

Uh oh, she thought. *Matthew had been naughty.*

She pocketed the letter and went back to work. At the end of the bed she found a storage cabinet. Inside of that, she found her prize: Matthew Hopkins' leather journal, his initials carved into the front.

Though she knew she probably needed to wait for John Gaule, she couldn't resist. She set down her candle and flipped through the journal.

And gasped.

At first she did not understand what she was seeing. But then, after flipping through the numerous pages, she put the puzzle together.

And it explained everything.

Hopkins and Gaule sat together in relative silence. Gaule finally broke it, tipping his mug. "Never thought we'd be doing this again, huh?"

"I am *very* tired, Mr. Gaule. Please just tell me what you need to so I may retire in peace."

"Wouldn't we all want that?" Gaule smiled. "For you to retire in peace. Never bother us again."

"This meeting's over." Hopkins stood angrily and started back toward his room.

"Your father wouldn't be proud!" Gaule shouted.

Hopkins stopped. He turned around.

"That is why you do what you do, yes?" Gaule asked. "To make daddy proud?"

"Been talking to my brother, have you?"

"Everyone talks, Matthew." Gaule took a sip of beer. "But sometimes you have to *really* listen, to understand what they are trying to say."

"And what did my brother say, exactly?"

Gaule knew he was getting to him. Truthfully, he had said *nothing* to his brother. He'd never even met the man. But Gaule, in his two decades of speaking to people through confession booths, had learned a thing or two about human nature. It was the most broken ones, he realized one day, that often felt they had the most to prove. And Hopkins struck Gaule as a man who felt he had a lot to prove.

"Your brother," Gaule said, "fears what his brother has become. And knows that your dear father would never be able to handle seeing you like this. Look at yourself, Matthew. The name Hopkins had once inspired hope, but now it just instills fear. Please. End this. You can still save your name. And your soul."

Hopkins was silent for a long, long time. But finally, and disappointingly, he let out a laugh. "That's the best you've got?"

Gaule shrugged. "My best shot."

"Never go into theater, Gaule. Your acting is terrible."

"The point remains, Matthew. Your father was an honorable man of God. What would he think of this?"

"You're not going to get the answer you want, Gaule," Hopkins sneered. "But I will give you an answer. He. Would. Be. *Proud.*"

Gaule glanced up to see Rebecca West quickly peer over the railing. Hopkins hissed something at Gaule then turned up the stairs. Rebecca West passed him and he gave her a vague look of recognition before letting her by.

"Matthew," Gaule shouted up at Hopkins.

Hopkins turned and gave him a final, hard stare.

"Never go into theater, either."

Hopkins waved him off and disappeared into his room, slamming the door shut. Moments later, there was a cry of panic from his room. This was accompanied by the sound of boxes and bags being flung about. Finally, Hopkins opened the door and emerged onto the balcony, looking enraged. He scanned the lobby, looking for Gaule and Rebecca West. When he didn't see them, he kicked open the door to the room next door.

It was empty.

Some ways down the street, in the attic of an old woman's house, Rebecca and John Gaule sat around a small candlelight. Gaule had known the woman for many years and had made lunch with her on several occasions during his trips through Ipswich. Earlier in the day, she had agreed to hide Gaule and Rebecca from Hopkins.

Rebecca had been apprehensive, fearing that the woman would turn them in. Gaule asked her to have faith, and luckily for both of them, it had been rewarded. When Matthew Hopkins banged on the door to the woman's home as he searched every building in town for Gaule and Rebecca, the woman told him that she had never heard of them and even offered to let him look around. That moment, if Gaule was being honest, scared him. Luckily, Hopkins didn't call the woman's bluff and moved on to the next house.

In the attic, Gaule caught his breath. Rebecca did not seem the least bit concerned as she sat cross-legged in front of the candle and handed Gaule the journal she had stolen from Hopkins' room.

"I also found this letter, from parliament," Rebecca handed Gaule the worn letter.

He looked over it. "Very interesting."

Apparently, Hopkins had indeed drawn the attention of parliament, enough so that they were actually requesting he come to London to "validate" his techniques. Apparently this didn't sit well with the man. And Hopkins' journal would unveil why.

As Gaule prepared to open it, Rebecca's rat appeared on her shoulder. He kept forgetting the thing existed until it appeared again. And it made him jump every time.

"Don't be frightened," Rebecca said. "He knows you're a good man at this point." She pet the rat. "He would've bit you if you weren't."

"I'm honored." Gaule rolled his eyes. "It's still just a bit weird of a pet, that's all."

"Ah, a lecture on being weird from a man who carries around exploding pebbles in his pocket."

"For science."

"I'm sure." She nodded to the journal. "Open it. It's...not quite what I was expecting."

"I'm expecting handwritten tips on how to deal with witches and possibly the secret to what makes Matthew Hopkins tick. If it's anything less, I'll be disappointed." Opening the journal, Gaule quickly cycled through its pages, his eyes lighting up.

It hadn't been handwritten tips on how to deal with witches. But it did reveal the secret that Matthew Hopkins had been hiding from all eyes other than his own.

Gaule, needless to say, was *not* disappointed.

-15-
ANGEL FLAMES

SEPTEMBER 1645

ONE DAY AFTER THE ARREST OF MARY LAKELAND

Morning. The insects, frogs and birds that had made Ipswich their home hummed to life. Sunlight streamed in through the metal bars of Mary Lakeland's prison cell, where together with the teenage Alice Denham, she was awakened by a guard. He was accompanied by one of the magistrates.

"Alice Denham and Mary Lakeland," the magistrate said. "We have come to a decision."

Downstairs, in the reception area of the magistrate's office, John Gaule argued with the clerk. "I have to see your superior! It's important!"

"It does not look important," the clerk replied, flipping through Hopkins' journal. "I do not even understand this."

"That belongs to Matthew Hopkins. And it proves that those women are innocent!"

"How?"

John Gaule explained the importance of the journal and its mysterious contents. The clerk still did not understand. Gaule was getting frustrated now. He knew the lives of Alice Denham and Mary Lakeland were at stake.

Little did he know, that just outside, they were indeed at stake...quite literally.

Rebecca turned her attention away from the men as they argued incoherently behind her. She stepped through the door, onto the sidewalk, and looked on as Alice Denham and Mary Lakeland were tied, back to back, against a pole in front of the town church. A crowd had gathered around to watch officials toss straw around the women, creating a mound so high that it nearly touched their knees.

Alice Denham screamed and squirmed. Her face was red with tears. An official silenced her by tying a cloth around her head, covering her mouth. Somehow, Rebecca thought, it made it worse. Now, instead of shrill screams, she could hear only the muffled crying of the girl no older than herself.

Mary Lakeland had been more resigned to her fate. She didn't even protest. Instead, she just slumped forward. Nonetheless, the officials gagged her as well. If only as a precautionary measure against what happened next.

While Gaule, oblivious to what was happening outside, continued to argue with the clerk, Rebecca stared in a trance as the women's bodies were doused with thick, black tar. Meanwhile, off to the side, a minister read last rites. When he had finished, the women were covered in so much tar that it was astonishing they hadn't drowned.

More straw was applied. Not at their feet, however, but on their bodies. Officials covered the women in straw, which stuck to the tar like glue, until they were barely recognizable as people anymore. Instead, they just looked like husks, like shells, like dolls made of straw.

When the fire was lit, the two women were immediately engulfed in the beastly flame. Even with the muzzles, their terrified screams of pain ripped through Rebecca's ears. It continued on for what felt like an eternity, before finally fading. The screams were replaced by the pops of their flesh and fat. As they melted, and their flesh sloughed away, the bones of their shoulders burned bright and hot. In the fire, Rebecca thought, they looked like angels.

"Don't look, child!" John Gaule, having realized what was happening, covered Rebecca's eyes. "Don't look." He held Rebecca close and began to pray under his breath.

The fire took only a few minutes to go out. When it was over, the smoldering remains of the stake and the charred bodies tied to it resembled a dead tree, the smoke of its soul ascending into the heavens.

"He's not getting away with this," Gaule seethed, suddenly filled with anger. "I'm ending this. *Now.*"

Gaule left Rebecca behind and took off in a full

sprint toward the Windward Inn. He pushed through patrons and grabbed a dinner knife off a table as he rushed upstairs. When he reached the top, he gripped the knife tight and *kicked* in the door to Mathew Hopkins' room.

It was empty.

He tossed over blankets and threw open drawers. Looking for something. Anything. He was blinded by fury.

"He's gone," Rebecca West said, leaning against the doorframe. "He's left, John."

Gaule took deep breaths. He dropped the knife, letting it clank on the floor. He exhaled. "He has to be stopped."

"Are you going to keep chasing him?" Rebecca asked.

"Someone has to."

"There are other ways, you know."

"I'm all out of mercy."

"Nonsense, you're a man of God." Rebecca walked in and closed the door behind her. She spoke in a calm, almost motherly voice as Gaule sat on the floor and slumped against a dresser. "Men of God,"

Rebecca said, "do not let rage guide them. A great man once told me that hate will only ensure more hate."

"What are you saying?" Gaule asked.

"Maybe it's time to go home. To Great Staughton."

"While Hopkins kills again?"

"Hopkins is a rabid dog. A dying one, John. He's by himself now. Parliament is on to him."

John Gaule nodded. "Maybe you're right. Maybe I can do more damage with my pen than I ever could...with this." He looked at the dinner knife.

"You're a good man, John Gaule." Rebecca grabbed his hand. "I admittedly know very little about this world, or about life, but I know this to be a solid truth. Maybe the only truth I've ever really known."

"Thank you." Gaule sighed. "I just wish that I...I could have saved at least one."

"Hey." Rebecca touched his cheek and looked into his eyes. "You did."

Downstairs, there was commotion. Someone was shouting, "It's a miracle!"

Curiously, Gaule and Rebecca went to investigate when they looked outside to see a crowd had gathered around a tiny home near the water.

"What's going on?" Gaule asked the innkeeper.

"Not sure. Something about Edward Reade's boy. The one who that witch Lakeland had given all those boils and rashes to."

John and Rebecca exchanged curious looks then darted out into the crowd. They pushed their way to the front where Edward Reade emerged from the house, smiling brightly. Behind him came his son, Henry Reade. However, unlike the red mess of rashes that had been described to John Gaule, Henry Reade looked clear as day. Not a single mark adorned his body and he looked to be the picture of good health.

"The witch's curse," Edward Reade declared confidently, "has been lifted!"

-16-
DEAD TREES

AUGUST 1647

TWO YEARS LATER

John Gaule finished reading the letter from Matthew Hopkins. After the initial surprise, he laughed it off, crumpled it up, and tossed it in a bin near his desk.

"Well," Daniel asked, "what did it say?"

"He said he'd be paying us a visit, soon."

"And this, uh, this doesn't concern you?"

"Of course not." Gaule picked up a few other letters on his desk. He started opening them, glancing at them, then tossing them back. "Mr. Hopkins' activities slowed to a trickle months ago and he hasn't been seen since. Most likely crawled back to Manningtree after the last village told him to take a hike. He's not the bogeyman he once was. The killing of John Lowes was enough to scare most people off."

"When was the last time you saw him, exactly?" Daniel asked, crossing his arms. He could not hide the hint of concern in his voice.

"Oh, two years ago now, in Ipswich."

"Ah, the case of Mary Lakeland. Tell me, was it not convincing?" Daniel asked.

"Convincing?" Gaule stopped and peered at a letter that had gained his particular interest. "What do you mean?"

"The boy. His wounds healed after the witches had burned. And the woman's husband…he died on the same day she was arrested."

"*Accused* witches." Gaule shook his head. "The boy was twenty-two years old and had probably picked up some fever. I've seen kids his age look like death one morning and a ray of sunshine the next. Believe me, neither Lakeland nor Denham were witches. Her husband, from what I understand, had been ill for months. His death was just…convenient."

"So, you believe Hopkins has retired for good?"

"Yes. Reduced to sending out threatening letters. The final stages of a losing battle. I imagine he's burned his last witch. After parliament's crackdown, none of his malarkey will fly in the courts anymore. He'll be remembered as a crazy old psycho. Nothing more."

"As long as you are certain."

"I am." Gaule finished reading a letter from his dear Rebecca West. Apparently she was ready to celebrate her 18th birthday somewhere in Suffolk. When she finished, she was going to return to Great Staughton to continue her lessons.

Gaule smiled. He had taken in Rebecca West as a student shortly after Ipswich. She'd excelled, racing past her other pupils in nearly every category. She seemed to take great pride in outperforming the male students, in particular.

She worked at the church three seasons out of the year but spent her summers travelling. Every time, she'd come back with a different story about where she'd been or the people she'd met. The young woman, Gaule thought, was going to do remarkable things. He couldn't wait to see her again. She'd become like a daughter to him, the one he always wanted but was never blessed enough to have.

Perhaps, God was looking out for me after all.

John Gaule had met many people in his journey through life, but very few struck him as sweetly as Rebecca West. She, in his eyes, was really, truly, a *good* person. One of the few genuinely good people he'd ever met, in fact. This thought comforted him.

But he was wrong.

H alf a country away, Matthew Hopkins sat in his master suite at the Thorn Inn. The inn he had purchased over a decade ago had become so sparingly-used that it was falling apart from the inside, not much more structurally sound than the ruins of the numerous medieval castles that dotted England.

Outside, the wind howled. Rain drenched the little inn, leaking through the ceiling. Hopkins had been ill for weeks. His skin was pale. It was suggested that he had picked up tuberculosis. A weaker man may have succumbed, but Hopkins would not allow himself to go without a fight. Despite his crippling sickness, he pressed on, writing letters to parliament, to Gaule, to whoever would listen to his increasingly-delusional rants and raves.

When he was finished with his tour of East Anglia, 300 men and women had been sent by him to the gallows. Hundreds of sinners had been cleansed from the land. Yet still, he did not sleep soundly. Something had nibbled at his mind.

Something was still not right.

Hopkins had not spoken to another human being for nearly a month. Towns and villages no longer accepted his services. He had become an outcast, a symbol of dread with whom no one wanted to associate. He found solitude to be his only company, though he was now giving serious consideration to heading into town for a tonic to help with his illness.

He had hoped it would die down soon. But it hadn't. It had only gotten worse. He was worried that picking up anything else would be the end of his life as he knew it.

I have been a warrior of God, he thought.

He will not allow me to die of this.

He will not allow me to die alone.

As darkness settled over Manningtree, Hopkins took off his hat and prepared to go to sleep, hoping he'd eventually throw up whatever sickness was festering inside of him. But as he sat on his bed, he noticed something: a book on his nightstand.

His book.

It was the journal.

Shaking, he picked up the book and looked inside. Though he hadn't seen it in two years, since it was stolen in Ipswich, it was just as he had remembered it.

Every page was blank.

You must do what is necessary even at the cost of your soul, Matthew Hopkins heard the words of his father. *Your mission will cost innocent lives. But they will serve a higher purpose and be welcomed into God's kingdom.* Hopkins closed the journal of blank pages. He gulped. He remembered his father's final words. *You must restore balance. You must keep our faith in control. Even if it is through terror. Even if it is through fear. God...will...forgive...*

There was a *squeak* and Hopkins felt a small prick of pain. When he looked down, he saw a large gray rat scurry out from between his feet and make its way to the corner of the room, where a figure stood in the darkness.

"Who are you?!" Hopkins yelled into the shadows as he examined his arm in the spot where the rat had bit him.

There was already a red rash forming.

"I can be whatever you want me to be," came a female voice that Hopkins immediately recognized. "That's what people do, right? They see what they want to see? They believe what they want to believe?"

The figure stepped forward, into the ray of moonlight that streamed in from the fractured ceiling. Rebecca West, with that sweet smile of hers, stared down Hopkins, who suddenly felt even sicker.

"You…" he whispered. "*You* stole my journal."

"I'd hardly call it a journal." Rebecca chuckled. "More like a prop. To get people to see what you wanted them to see. Dunking. Pissing in bottles. Shoes in chimneys. You were making all of this up as you went along, pretending it was in some book." She shook her head. "You clever son of a bitch."

Hopkins smirked. "You caught me."

"You got smart, too." Rebecca smiled. "The trick with the priest, John Lowes. You held on to the winch and kept him above the water, then slowly lowered him down until he confessed. And you got away with it because no one was looking at you."

"I actually feel bad about the priest," Hopkins said. "But I needed to send a message to your friend, John Gaule. I'd say one life was worth the cost." Hopkins started to feel woozy. He looked down at the rat bite on his arm. Something very strange was happening to it...it seemed to be changing shape right before his eyes.

"I know a thing or two about feeling bad about killing," Rebecca West said. "I do still feel a bit guilty about the child..."

And just like that, everything came into focus. The bite on Hopkins' arm had formed the shape of a six-ended star. An asterisk.

Just like what had been seen on John Rivet's child.

And on Henry Reade.

And on his own father.

"You!" Hopkins exclaimed, feeling faint. "It was you! *Your rat killed the Rivet child!*"

"Hey, hey, I didn't *ask* him to do anything. He was foraging, and the child scared him with his cries. Most healthy people are strong enough to fight off the infection that comes with his bite. Henry Reade was young and strong. It vanished after a day." The rat climbed up on her shoulder. She pet it gently. "But an infant is too weak to fight."

Hopkins felt his legs give out beneath him. He fell to the floor, crawling on his stomach, struggling to breathe.

Rebecca West knelt down in front of him. "You really are a pathetic creature, you know?"

"*Fuck you*, witch!" Dribble had begun to fall from Hopkins' mouth.

Rebecca shrugged. "Don't be silly. Witches use magic. I prefer something in between."

"Henry Reade…my father…how did you…"

"Mine isn't the only rat in the world nor does it have the only infectious bites." Rebecca laughed. "Or perhaps there are some who are just angry Familiars, now lost because their host witches have been killed by one Matthew Hopkins, the Witchfinder General."

"You're lying...you're a witch..."

Rebecca smiled. She reached down and tilted Hopkins' weakened head up so she could meet his gaze. "A great man once told me that there is no more dangerous combination than ego and ignorance."

As she spoke, the walls seemed to slowly start to come to life. There appeared to be movement behind them. And sounds. Hopkins thought he was hallucinating.

Rebecca continued, "And you, Mr. Hopkins, are the living embodiment of both. All of this world's evils are caused by men like you. Ones who believe that this is their world and that we must follow by their rules. But I have something to tell you, Mr. Hopkins."

Rebecca leaned forward as Hopkins struggled for breath. She closed her eyes and kissed him on the forehead. "This is not your world."

Squeaks emanated from the walls. Then, like a deluge, dozens, if not hundreds of rats emerged from the rotting wood of the inn and began to converge on Matthew Hopkins.

"It's *mine*."

Rebecca stood and watched with a cold gaze as Matthew Hopkins was swallowed by the sea of rats. His screams were muffled and he writhed and struggled. She jammed her foot onto the back of his neck and held him in place as the rodents went to work, chomping off pieces of flesh, bit by bit, wearing the man down to a skeleton.

"And I intend to do with it as I please, Mr. Hopkins," Rebecca said as she removed her foot from the writhing mass of creatures below her. She couldn't even see Hopkins anymore. He was trapped beneath a hundred rats, screaming as they picked away at his body.

Rebecca West didn't want to watch the man end. She left the room and closed the door, hearing his screams slowly fade as she descended the stairs of the inn and walked out. By the time she stepped outside, she could hear nothing but the rain hammering the inn. She opened her hands and dropped some chunks of spare bait on the ground. Almost immediately, rats began to emerge from the ground to feast.

He will die thinking I'm a witch.

Skipping happily toward her horse, Rebecca

climbed on and then let it take her down the road, away from Manningtree. She sang as her horse galloped through the foggy countryside that, even in the summer, was dotted with the remnants of dead trees.

"The enemy threw him over, for on the deck he died. It was here the man drifted, with the flow of the tide. And sank to the bottom, of the Lowland Sea. Because he refused to give up, his Golden Vanity."

ILLUSTRATIONS

An illustration of Matthew Hopkins from the 1837
edition of his book, *The Discovery of Witches*.

Matthew Hopkins interrogating Elizabeth Clarke, surrounded by her Familiars. From the cover of the first edition of *The Discovery of Witches* (1647).

An accused witch is subjected to dunking.

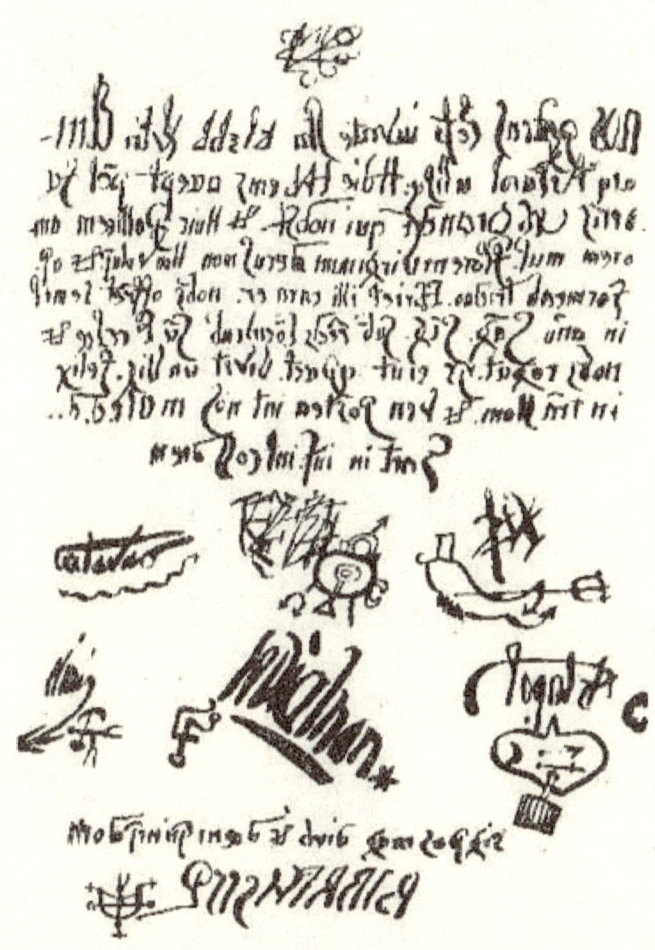

A typical "contract" with the Devil used as evidence against Urbain Grandier in 1634. Though an obvious forgery, Grandier was still burned at the stake.

DÆMONOLOGIE,
IN FORME
OF A DIA-
LOGVE,

Diuided into three books:

WRITTEN BY THE HIGH
and mightie Prince, IAMES by the
grace of God King of England,
Scotland, France *and* Ireland,
Defender of the Faith, &c.

LONDON,
Printed by *Arnold Hatfield* for
Robert Wald-graue,
1 6 0 3

The title page of *Daemonologie* as it may have
appeared to Matthew Hopkins.

ABOUT THE AUTHOR

Brent Saltzman was born on July 29, 1988 in Fairfax, VA. He graduated from Radford University in 2011.